William Frederick Rock

Poems: Winter Gatherings

William Frederick Rock

Poems: Winter Gatherings

ISBN/EAN: 9783337207090

Printed in Europe, USA, Canada, Australia, Japan

Cover: Foto ©Andreas Hilbeck / pixelio.de

More available books at **www.hansebooks.com**

WINTER GATHERINGS.

BY

WILLIAM FREDERICK ROCK.

𝔏𝔬𝔫𝔡𝔬𝔫:

W. KENT AND CO., PATERNOSTER ROW.

MDCCCLXXVII.

UNWIN BROTHERS, PRINTERS, CHILWORTH AND LONDON.

PREFACE.

TEN years ago I printed for private circulation an edition of my verses, the whole of which has been long since presented to my friends. I have since had many solicitations for further copies, and I almost feel bound to meet these complimentary applications by a reprint. This has led to my now placing the volume before the public, and I shall doubtless soon learn whether I have done well or otherwise in letting any of my writings go beyond the pleasant circle of my friends.

W. F. R.

HYDE CLIFF, BLACKHEATH,
    September, 1877.

CONTENTS.

POEMS.

CONTENTS.

POETIC SITES.

CONTENTS.

FLOWERS.

CONTENTS.

SONGS.

CONTENTS.

POEMS.

THE BLIND MAN.

FEELING his way with tapping stick,
And steps as slow as mine were quick,
I saw an old grey-headed man,
And thus I hailed him as I ran :
" Halloo ! my old blind friend, I pray
Move onward, do not stop the way."

"I am not blind," said the old man;
"I once was blind, and then I ran ;
But since I saw I ran too quick,
I take to walking with a stick."

" Oh fie, old greybeard, blindman, fie,
I do not like to hear a lie
Even in sport and from the young ;
But oh, how black is falsehood, hung
On a slow-moving, aged tongue !"

2

"Sweet youth," replied the tottering sage,
"Thy words revive my drooping age.
Come seat me down."   And then he sighed
And said, "Sit by an old man's side,
And he will tell what 'tis to be
Stone-blind, and what it is to see.

"In days long past I ranged the fields
(What boundless pleasure nature yields!)
The vermeil-fringèd daisies sprung
Close to my feet when I was young,
And yellow buttercups were spread
In rich profusion 'neath my tread;
Glowing dog-roses every bush
Made beauteous with their crimson blush;
The hawthorn bloom decked each May bough
With floral silver just as now;
On every bank, o'er all the ground,
Nature spread loveliness around,
She clothed with beauty every spot,
And yet, alas, I saw it not!
I did not see the swallow come
Each summer to its English home;
I heard no music from the air,
Nor marked the soaring skylark there;
Flowers, birds, and all the merry things
That fly about with buzzing wings,

So full of love's blest melody,
All these, alas ! were lost on me :
I saw them not !   You show surprise !
But for all these I had no eyes."

" O father, father, do not speak
Like this, or else my heart will break.
Alas ! how dimly have I seen !
I scarcely know that fields are green ;
The wingèd music of the sky
I've heeded not, yet know not why ;
Like yours, my morn is almost night ;
Oh tell me how you got your sight ! "

" My dear young man, it pleasèd God
To chasten me with His mild rod ;
The eyes that were no use to me
He closed, and I BEGAN TO SEE !
I never moved my stilled eyelid,
Yet saw each flower that once was hid ;
I thought on all the loveliness
Which bloomed when I admired it less ;
I paced (in mind) by every hedge,
Lifted each russet tuft of sedge,
Thought on the violets which breathe
Their fragrance from the moss beneath ;

Looked up, as if I could see there
The lark sustained in upper air ;
Thought of the beauty of each nook ;
Read the first page of Nature's book ;
Turned my thoughts round this happy ball
Of earth where constant blessings fall,
And a God's goodness saw in all.

" O happy, ever happy day,
When, moistened with the mystic clay,
My eyes first opened to light's ray ;
There is no blindness half so blind
As the cold darkness of the mind,
Which passing through a lovely world,
Sees beauty's banner half unfurled ;
Which sees the sun pass through the skies,
Or knows that it must set and rise ;
Sees the blest summer and the spring
Give warmth to every living thing ;—
Which views all this, though seen so plain,
With cold neglect, or bold disdain.
O my dear friend, to you is left
The light of which I am bereft ;
Kneel down with me and we will pray :
Grant us, O God, Thy heavenly ray,
That, our eyes opened, we may see
In every good a type of Thee ;

That we may look around and trace
Thy bounteous hand in every place,
And then raise eyes and hearts above,
And thus repay Thee love for love."

THE COTTAGER'S ADDRESS TO THE MORNING STAR.

" Behold, the sun, and the moon, and the eleven stars made obeisance
to me."—GEN. xxxviii. 9.

STAR of the morning, tellest thou of day ?
Sweet is the visit of thy silvery ray.
    A gentle bud of light,
    More beautiful than bright,

Thou light'st the path of the pale dawn's first hours,
Liftest the drooping eyelids of the flowers,
    And breathest musical words
    To wake the sleeping birds.

I hear their chirpings from the leafy wood,
A twitter first, and then a swelling flood
    Of gratitude to Him
    Who claims their morning hymn.

Delicious Star ! Thy twinkling from above
Awakes the flowers to smiles, the birds to love ;
    And when all else has smiled,
    Thou call'st thy favourite child.

Then Man awakes !   The sovereign of the whole,
Creation's lord, the creature with a soul !
  He wakes to life—to thought
  Which worlds could not have bought.

He wakes, and looks around, below, above ;
All is for him, and all is bright with love,
  And his swoll'n heart is full,
  All is so beautiful.

And then he wonders at creation's plan :
Who could have formed the earth, and seas, and man?
  And his knee meets the sod,
  While his lips breathe forth "God !"

Yet thought will wander, and he heaves a sigh
At the reflection that he still must die,
  And all this beauty leave
  Perhaps before the eve.

Still, thought flows on.   Yes, man indeed will fade,
Returning to the dust whence he was made ;
  But wherefore should he sigh?
  His soul can never die.

Star of the Morning, shine, and wane and shine,
More fixed than thou, eternity is mine :
  Yés, Man is nobler far
  E'en than the Morning Star !

THE COTTAGER'S ADDRESS TO THE EVENING STAR.

"The star that bids the shepherd fold."—MILTON.

BRIGHT Evening Star! my harbinger of rest,
The spot where thou first twinklest must be blest :
        My own dear family sun,
        My toil I see is done.

Blest star, if worlds indeed around thee move,
They must be worlds of bliss—be worlds of love ;
        For rest to us thou bringest,
        And love's sweet song thou singest.

At thy first glimmer in the soft'ning sky,
Brown Labour smiles and lays his mattock by ;
        And Youth looks up to see
        The eye of love in thee.

When the bright beams of day begin to leave
For the soft twilight of the love-fraught eve,
        Spell-bound, I scarce can turn
        From where thy beauties burn.

At thy calm smile the city's voice grew dim,
The little lark, too, ceased its vesper hymn,
    And Echo, in its pride,
    Repeated it and died.

Silence is born of thee, and speech is still,
Though eloquence the bursting heart may fill;
    The voice of love alone,
    Sweet sparkler, is thine own.

Thou shinest o'er thy cotter's home, blest star,
Where all his hopes and all his pleasures are;
    All but one spot is dim
    To point that out to him.

A needless task; for what is all beside
The tender pleasures of our own fireside?
    What luxury, what bliss,
    To have a spot like this!

My wife's sweet welcome at my cottage door,
My little prattlers meeting me before,
    What more can riches give?
    The richest can but live.

Shine, lovely one! Oh, twinkle as before,
And though thou canst not give thy cotter more.
    Shine on, and mayst thou see
    Each cotter blest like me!

PARADISE TREE.

(NEAR BIDEFORD, DEVON.)

" Not only famous, but of that *good* fame
Without which glory's but a tavern song."—BYRON.

How many a summer's sun
Has danced thy leaves upon !
How often the night zephyrs, sighing,
Have set thy green honours a-flying !
    For a tree more fair
    Never waved in the air,
Nor perhaps more gracefully twined a bough,
Than thine, so shrivelled and wrinkled now.

There garlands perhaps have hung,
And woodland songsters sung,
And lovers have sat and sighed
That the moon its beam might hide,
    And a moment's relief
    To darken thy leaf
Has been seized on by them for a rapturous kiss,
No witness but thou to their innocent bliss.

Perhaps thou wert part of a wood,
And hast all thy tall neighbours outstood,

And while, like " the lords of the ground,"
They were nodding and falling around,
    The roots of thy birth
    Grew more fast to the earth;
And, though not so green, thou art standing as stern
As if thou wert still unexpecting thy turn.

I can fancy that under thy shade
The pipe and the fiddle have played,
While round thee in fairy-like ring
The youth of the village would fling;
    For fame must be wrought,
    Or 'tis quickly forgot;
And how many a heart must have bounded with glee
To earn thee the sweet name of " PARADISE TREE !"

Oh, that story, old Stump, should withhold
These tales of the pleasures of old !
If the joys of these times are so few,
Come, give us the old ones anew,
    Or I in my rhyme
    Will sing of the time
When the lads and the lasses at eve came to thee,
And danced in the shade of old Paradise Tree.

" I was reared then "—Hark ! hark ! " I was reared—
But age has my memory seared;

Yet many have shaken my bough
Whose faces I never see now,
    And I tremble to hear
    The names still so dear,
Now talked of as heading a funeral stone,
While the villagers weep for my friends that are gone.

" I have heard the soft sighs of the heart,
I have felt of each sorrow a part,
I have heard the loud laugh 'neath my boughs,
Which shook with the joyous carouse ;
    The wanderer's feet
    Have turned to my seat,
And in storm and in sunshine for ever were free
The shade and the shelter of Paradise Tree.

" I've administered oft to the mirth
Of the village to which I owe birth ;
Given shade 'mid the summer day's toil,
And added at eve to their smile ;
    Nor did I withhold,
    When the winter blew cold,
A straggling branch from the shivering poor,
And what could the Lord of the Manor do more ?

" My young boughs have waved in the air
When beauty and freshness were there,

And now, when the wintry wind
Has bleached and disfigured my rind,
    Enjoying the fame
    Of a time-honoured name,
I can smile at the crowds who only are known
By their name on a moss-covered mouldering stone.

"But what shall I say to the one
Who admires me when beauty has gone,
When the dark howling wintery blast
Has withered my top as it passed?
    I have nought to repay,
    For I fall to decay,
But softly my ashes shall crumble o'er thee,
If they bury thee under old Paradise Tree."

A DAY AT INSTOW, DEVON.

I SPENT a day, oh! such a day,
Why will such moments pass away?
Pure joy, I think, should ever stay.

I was in Devon, on the marge
Of two clear rivers; neither large,
Their freshets scarcely float a barge.

But each can boast a foaming tide
So deep that safely there may ride
Large ships, the mighty ocean's pride.

Wild Dartmoor gives one stream its source ;
Wending round pleasant woods its course,
From each hill-brook it gathers force.

The TAW, my own loved native stream,
Is worth a water-poet's dream ;
It is a floating sunshine beam.

Whether it lifts its tiny moans
In leaping over boulder stones,
Or tinkles with more silver tones ;

Or passing Tawstock's verdant wood,
At Barum meets the upward flood,
And shows the town its river god.

Child of the moor, the TORRIDGE, too,
At first as small as dropping dew,
Soon soaks a crystal passage through

The bog, the sheep-paths, the roadside,
(Where sunburnt maidens ponies ride,)
And finds its daisied margin wide.

For having left its ridgy Tors,
And the adjoining sheep-cropped moors,
It soon its rain-fed ripples pours,

And gives its name to a fair town ;
Then, wider spreading, topples down
Through grassy meads in channels brown.

Still wider grown, the Torridge rill,
Passing Weir Gifford's manse and mill,
Takes shadows from Malclevi's hill.

Then leaves its rural banks of sedge,
And leaping Ford's old stepping-ridge,
Sweeps through the many archèd bridge.

Well—these two streams, their wanderings o'er,
Just as they go, to be no more,
Join their bright floods at Appledore.

And opposite that port marine,
At once a sea and sylvan scene,
Sits INSTOW, like a river queen ;

Rich in its sands and fishers' hooks,
And daisied hills and cottage nooks,
As poets will describe, in books.

There our dear " Invalided" lay,
And wrote us how that day by day
Health chased her pallid looks away.

And so I said, "Well, I will go
Where these health-bearing breezes blow ;
I'm off!—aye, whether I can or no."

I Instow reached and smiled, and said,
"God bless you, the pale cheeks are fled,
And once again, dear, they are red :

And as you are not very weak,
And I have only just a week,
Each day we must some pleasure seek."

But this I scarcely need have said,
For plans enough were ready laid,
Though I a dozen weeks had stayed.

Well, for our day.   We rose at seven,
And saw, of course, a sunny heaven,
For which and all, our thanks were given.

I, before breakfast, sallied forth,
And knew the place from south to north,
And every man's and woman's worth.

Then, after coffee, milk, and eggs,
And thin-sliced tongue, and chicken's legs,
We filled the hamper and the kegs.

And at that moment came along
Our boatman, with a snatch of song ;
With him the wind is never wrong.

" Well, William ! how about the boat ? "
" Plaise, Mim, 'tis jist agot afloat,
An' I've the oars an' zails abrought."

Ten minutes placed us in our seats,
And in the midships drinks and meats,
And little knick-knacks, fruits and sweets.

And, as we wished, the fair winds blew,
And as we tacked the winds tacked too,
Just as they usually do.

With pleasant tales and hearty joys,
And laughs, and songs, and such sweet noise,
We passed by all the pilot buoys.

William declared a sweet-toned gale
From every song swelled out his sail
(Such winds at Instow must prevail).

Full soon " the pebble ridge " we reach :
Running our shallop on the beach,
We landed with a load for each.

Piling our stores on the sand-banks,
We then began to play our pranks,
Through drifted sand and tall sedge ranks ;

Now looking at a dark sea-mew,
Now listening to the wild curlew,
Or stepping little sea-pools through.

And then we gathered tiny cells
Of sea things, many coloured shells,
Thrown up from ocean's briny wells ;

And wondered why such lovely forms
Were given as houses for such worms ;
And talked of calms and talked of storms.

And then leaped over rifted rocks,
And stranded rudders, yards, and blocks,
And saved a bit to make a box.

And every now and then we met
Sea-dabs and weeds above the wet,
And varied stones, from milk to jet.

And searching, as we sauntered on,
We now and then selected one,
And thought the last the brightest shone.

And here and there we caught a glimpse
In rock-pools of those little imps,
The savoury morsels we call shrimps.

And then I said, " You here may rest,
Until I yonder am undrest :
I will the foamy ocean breast.

" Five minutes will be ample quite,
I shall be nearly out of sight,
And only seem a speck of white.

" Then see me in the salt sea lave,
And battle with the mountain wave,
And talk of manhood and the brave."

Well ! this passed too.   We look abroad,
And see along the sandy road
Our boatman struggling with his load.

We run, with pleasure in our eyes,
And each a little help supplies,
And soon unpacked are joints and pies.

Stones form our table and our seat,
Pebbles confine our napkin neat ;
And thus might princes drink and eat.

Then on the sand supine we lie,
Looking right up into the sky,
All thoughtless and luxuriously ;

Just deeming that those pretty things
That bask in sunbeams their gauze wings,
Might lessons give to queens and kings.

But this, you know, would only do
Just for a warm half-hour or two,
Not for the afternoontide through.

So after just a little snooze,
We thought us of our homeward cruise,
And even hinted evening's dews.

William had left us but light work ;
We packed each napkin, knife and fork,
And played at balls with every cork.

But ere we left the hallowed ground,
One song from each was sung around,
And off we sprang with merry bound.

3 *

Since then, in London's noisiest throng,
The echo of each simple song
Oft floats the busy din among.

Distinct above the varied noise
Which marks the struggle for life's toys,
It sings, " How cheap are harmless joys !"

THE RUINED TEMPLE.

" He spake of the temple, his body."
" The temple of the Lord is holy, which temple ye are."

Look at yon fane where ruin sits,
Where serpents twine and the bat flits,
Where noxious weeds grow high and rank,
Concealing pits obscene and dank.

This was a temple fair and bright,
Glowing with pure and heavenly light,
A temple of the living God,
Which nothing base or sinful trod.

Once holy love and fervent prayer
From morn till silent night were there,
And every virtue of the mind
Was in this temple once enshrined.

There dwelt the ever-blessed three,
Pure Faith, and Hope, and Charity ;
And God Himself, with special grace,
Made it His own bright dwelling-place.

O favoured temple ! glorious shrine !
O dwelling-place thus made divine !
What ruined thus the bright abode
Of the supreme, eternal God ?

In evil hour a fatal sin
Knocked at the door and entered in,
And spread around its loathsome breath,
Drawn from the charnel-house of death.

The power of darkness chased away
The shining spirits of the day ;
Faith, Hope, and Charity all fled,
And left Despair and Hate instead.

Then love in lust unholy burned,
And soberness to riot turned,
And stern defiance, doubts and fears
Came, but no penitential tears.

The *oratory* gave no sigh,
But deep-mouthed oath or ready lie ;
The *altar* had its garlands torn,
Which were as sinful trophies worn.

The *lattice*, whence Love used to look,
Unholier spirits conquering took ;
The *Tower of Heshbon* tumbling came,
Pulled down by Guilt's debasing shame.

What could the Great Eternal do,
But, still to purest virtue true,
Leave the foul ruin as it fell,
To the congenial powers of hell ?

High o'er the ruin Satan cowers,
The fatal conquest of his powers,
Boasts of a temple won from heaven,
And to his dread dominion given.

The howl of darkness and despair
Thence pours to him a fitting prayer,
And brimstone censers there he lights,
In mockery of holier rites.

But Mercy, from its bright abode,
Stoops, with an offer yet from God ;
Awakens Hope, still lingering there,
Which whispers in it yet a prayer.

'Twas but for mercy, one deep sigh,
But see ! Despair and Anguish fly :
The temple's echoing walls are full—
"The Lord our God is merciful ! "

The holy altar smokes again,
Not with the blood of bullocks slain ;
A contrite heart upon it lies,
And God accepts the sacrifice.

O wondrous temple ! living fane !
Bright dwelling-place of God again !
Thence daily shall fresh incense rise,
With prayer and penitential sighs.

Till, consecrate in perfect love,
Incorporate with thy church above,
Restored, this temple, Lord, shall be ;
Builded, raised up, and blent with Thee.

THE ENCHANTER'S GLASS.

COME, come, Enchanter, prithee pass
The earth's bright phantoms o'er thy glass ;
Come, show me what the world can give
To one who wishes well to live.
    The scene is sweet ;—a joyous child ;
Its crowing laugh, its tendril fingering,
    Like a young vine-shoot running wild,
Clinging to all, yet nowhere lingering.
O Childhood ! happy, blithe, and free,
I will choose thee ; yes, I'll choose thee.

Yet pass this scene.　Thou canst show more,
Enchanter, by thy magic lore ;
Prithee my pulse more wildly move
With deeper scenes.　I would see Love.
　　What's this?　Ah ! love indeed is here ;
No one can doubt that faithful greeting,
　　Its joy, its still more precious tear,
The tear of parting—aye, of meeting,
When love's cup overflows with bliss.
I will choose this ; I will choose this.

Again shift on thy figures, Seer,
The world's great gifts do not appear ;
I would view one who has been hurled
Amidst the bustling busy world.
　　I see !　Yon struggler leaps and tries
To reach the golden prize hung o'er him ;
　　He gains it !　See, the good and wise
Bow down their care-bleached heads before him.
'Tis well—how can it be amiss
To o'ertop all ?—I will choose this.

Thy shadows, Seer, again pass on,
I still would see a nobler one,
One who can boast a titled name
High on the glittering roll of fame.

Ah ! there he is ! without a scar,
He has the homage of a nation,
   A medal, garter, cross, and star—
The highest rank, the proudest station.
Well, this *is* brave.   No one, I wis,
Can e'er condemn if I choose this.

O Seer, my weary spirits pant
For something I seem yet to want;
The little phantoms of thy glass
Are all forgotten as they pass.
   What is this scene?   In bold relief
A bowed-down figure I am seeing,
   A man of sorrows and of grief.
O God ! it is that Precious Being;
Sorrow with Him appears such bliss,
I will choose this, I will choose this.

Sorrow for sin.   There is no part,
In earthly or in heavenly heart,
So good, so Godlike, or so pure,
So bright, so lasting, or so sure.
   But whence these tears in Him who spread
The great and glorious heaven above me ?
   Oh, can it be?   His tears thus shed
Because I sin.   Can He still love me?
Oh let me mingle mine with His !
SORROW FOR SIN.   I will choose this !

"*IT IS I, BE NOT AFRAID.*"

CEASE, timid soul, each agonizing sigh,
    Be every fear, be every doubt allayed;
Dread not the storm which howls along the sky,
The Spirit that controls the storm is nigh.
                        " 'Tis I, be not afraid ! "

Does sin assail, thy wavering faith to try;
    By Me, thy Staff, thy fallings shall be stayed;
Look but on Me, the evil one will fly;
Fear not, thou little one, for I am nigh.
                        " 'Tis I, be not afraid ! "

Say, hast thou fallen?   Thou meet'st no angry eye,
    Since thou repentest, I will not upbraid;
Enough one tear, one penitential sigh;
I knew the trial, how, and when, and why.
                        " 'Tis I, be not afraid ! "

Does sickness bow thee, does the grave seem nigh,
    Does heaven not brighten as earth 'gins to fade ?
Cheer up, poor doubter, time is passing by;
Repose in holy confidence—" 'Tis I."
                        " 'Tis I, be not afraid ! "

THE MONARCH'S ENTRY.

" Fear not, daughter of Zion, behold thy King cometh."—JOHN xii. 15.

LIFT up your head, great Salem's gate,
  Welcome your Victor-monarch home ;
The King of Jewry and His state
  In new and mighty triumph come !
Ten thousand voices move the air,
  And the loud plaudits fill the sky,
Ten thousand bosoms beat their prayer—
  Hosanna to the Lord most High !

The multitude have strewn the way
  As ne'er was Conqueror's pathway spread,
No boughs of laurel or of bay,
  Ensanguined types of life-blood shed ;
But the green palm-branch, speaking peace
  To all on earth, goodwill to men,
Tells of the time when war shall cease,
  And lambs lie in the lion's den.

The Victor comes ! His captives, see,
  Follow in meek array his train ;
His captives, those whom He makes free !
  Enfranchised souls from Satan's chain.

The proud, by meekness low subdued,
  In full submission now lie down ;
The meek, with holy hopes endued,
  Look up and ask and share His crown.

The blind whom He hath made to see,
  The lame whom He hath made to go,
His triumph join.   With new-born glee
  The lame man leapeth like the roe ;
The deaf awake to sounds unused,
  They hear the wide-resounding cry ;
The dumb speak out, their tongues now loosed,
  Hosanna to the Lord most High !

Jerusalem receives her King,
  The mighty Monarch mounts his throne,
Uplifted high !   Strange triumphing !
  For see, His sacred blood hath flown ;
Suspended on the fatal tree,
  In death His holy head bows down
In solitary majesty,
  For all His followers have flown.

He triumphs yet.   Borne to the tomb,
  The stone is sealed and watched in vain,
The grave itself is but the womb
  Whence God and man are born again.

Death hath surrendered now its sting,
   No more victorious is the grave,
A mightier realm now claims its King,
   A countless throng their Monarch crave.

The sky unwonted glory wears,
   Filled with a bright angelic train;
The new Jerusalem appears,
   And Jesus here is King again.
Lo! He ascends! Our eyes in vain
   Would view the wonders of above;
Commenced is the Eternal Reign,
   The Reign of Glory, Goodness, Love.

THE KIND MASTER.

"My yoke is easy, and my burden is light."—MATTHEW xi. 30.

I LOOK around upon the busy world,
   And see an anxious and a struggling throng
So sad, it seems as though a curse were hurled
   Upon each victim as he moves along.
The sunken eye, the wrinkled brow of care,
   The quivering lip and the upheaving breast,
The gasping breath, the ever-ready tear,
   The unsteady pulse, a stranger to all rest.

What breeds this tumult, and what means this din ?
  What demon guides them, or what tyrants drive ?
Can ill from good proceed ?   When days begin
  Must sin and sorrow with the light arrive ?
Alas ! man, self-enslaved, no more retains
  The mighty freedom of his early days ;
The slave of many masters hugs his chains,
  And pride and passion he by turns obeys :

Hard taskers they.   At their too stern demands
  Joy and Content take wing, e'en Wisdom flies.
At Mammon's altar, Truth a victim stands ;
  Virtue and Hope complete the sacrifice.
What is this idol-worship, that we bow
  Our abject forms to lick the monster's dust ?
Who thus delights to see his slaves so low?
  " The Good," " The Wise," " The Mighty," or " The
    Just " ?

Ah, no !   It is the god of *this* world claims
  Such fearful homage from his trembling slaves ;
'Tis Satan's vassals who thus work in chains,
  Till pain and anguish sink them to their graves.
Oh, can it be, that, deaf to reason's voice,
  From grace, from mercy, from redeeming love
Man turns away and makes a fatal choice,
  Grovelling below, when he might soar above ?

Another Master would his soul engage,
   The yoke is easy, and the burden light ;
Eternal glory is the offered wage,
   A home unfading and companions bright.
Come, sin-encumbered, throw thy burden down !
   Come, over-wearied, come to Him and rest !
The low, the abject yet may wear a crown ;
   The doomed, the fallen, the helpless yet be blessed !

He calls !   His gracious promises invite
   To joy, to happiness, the guilty throng ;
Serve Him with gladness, in His law delight,
   And come before His presence with a song.
No gloomy service His.   A joy supreme
   Pervades each heart that puts its trust in Him ;
Immortal goodness is the constant theme,
   Eternal praises the unceasing hymn.

Oh, come, be blest !   Risk not an hour's delay ;
   Leave this world's gods, idols of stock and stone,
With heads of gold and feet of miry clay,
   And serve the Lord Omnipotent alone !
The Great, the Gracious Giver of all good
   Withholds no bounty, and denies no care ;
For gifts, the Giver asks but gratitude,
   For hope, for grace, for mercy, but a prayer.

ROBIN OF AYR.

I HAD a blessèd dream last night ;
   I slept with moonbeams·for my pillows,—
Such moonbeams as, with silver light,
   Tip and smooth down the summer billows.
I lay, though soul-entranced, awake ;
   Or, if asleep, in softest slumbers ;
No spring-bird's music from the brake
   Could match my fancy's pleasant numbers :
      I heard my Robin, our own dear Robin,
      Our ricketty-racketty, own dear Robin !
No linnet or thrush, from blossoming bush,
   E'er sang like our own dear high-souled Robin.

I looked up and the sky was light,
   And full of happy, joyous creatures,
And 'mid the brightest of the bright
   I saw dear Robin's well-known features ;
Foremost among the glittering throng,
   He looked so white, and fair and pure,
I scarcely knew our child of song,
   He stood so calm and so demure.

But there was Robin, our own dear Robin,
　　Our ricketty-racketty, own dear Robin,
Not his daisy bright with its vermeill'd white
　　Could look more pure than our own dear Robin.

I said, " Why, Robert, can that be you ?
　　How came ye, my lad, that long white robe in ? "
Quoth he with a smile that quite warmed me through,
　　" From Time's first day it was made for Robin ;
The world only saw me in ploughman's dress,
　　Spattered and soiled by the crowd I moved in ;
It has since been cleaned of its mire and mess,
　　But it's the very robe I lived and loved in."
　　　　Oh, dear Robin ! loving Robin !
　　　　My ricketty-racketty, own dear Robin !
There's never a king that poet could sing
　　That had such a robe as this dear Robin !

" But how did you manage, dear Robert," said I,
　　" To atone for your faults ? You've been punished, I'm
　　　　thinking :
Very often folk say of you, Rob, with a sigh,
　　' Oh what has become of Rob's roving and drinking ?'"
Robin said : " Don't you know in this glorified sphere
　　There's no such debasement as tippling and roving,
Good fellowship turns to communion here,
　　And our constant employment is singing and loving.

Yes, your Robin, your own dear Robin,
The once so ricketty-racketty Robin,
Still sings the same tune, as by Ayr and by Doon,
He is still the same heart-throbbing, love-breathing
Robin!"

———

"*THIS IS AS IT SHOULD BE.*"

(THE LAST WORDS OF DOUGLAS JERROLD.)

THE time speeds on when we must go
From all who love us, all we love!
The hour will have its share of woe,
However blest the change may prove;
However bright heaven's opening skies,
Although we may both great and good be,
Affection's tears will dim the eyes,
And this is as it should be.

Oh, who unweeping and unwept
Would leave a world so fair as this,
Which when he woke and when he slept
Had still love's look, love's smile, love's kiss;
Where wife, child, sister, brother, friend
Were loving, aye, as fond hearts could be—
Love lasting on unto the end!
Oh this is as it should be!

Raised, gently raised by some kind hand,
    Leaning on some dear, loving breast,
Surrounded by the close-linked band,
    Our hand by some hand fondly pressed;
Hearing the half-suppressèd sighs,
    As gently breathed as anguish could be,
Looking on tear-suffusèd eyes;
    Oh this is as it should be !

O precious sighs ! O joyous tears !
    O grief that almost hallows feeling !
O glorious hopes ! O needful fears,
    Salvation's wondrous plan revealing !
Weep, dear ones ! weep as Jesus wept
    For one He loved. Wept let the good be,
But be not grief's bounds overstepped ;
    Let all be as it should be.

Come, sweet remembrances of all
    The tenderness which marked their living;
Yes, let our memories recall
    Our frequent faults, their warm forgiving :
Then one long thought, that they must now
    With countless myriads of the good be ;
That when we meet again, we know
    All will be as it should be.

"*NOW I SHALL GO TO SLEEP.*"

(THE LAST WORDS OF BYRON.)

" It was about six o'clock on the evening of this day when he said, ' Now I shall go to sleep,' and then turning round fell into that slumber from which he never awoke."—MOORE'S *Notices of the " Life of Byron."*

Now I shall go to sleep.   Oh yes, my day of life is o'er ;
The sun which shortly now will set will rise to me no
    more ;
What I have earned I now shall gain, what I have sown
    shall reap ;
I cannot add unto my work, now I shall go to sleep.

If I have never done as I would others did to me,
Or if unheeded I have heard the voice of misery,
If I have caused the orphan's sigh or made the widow
    weep,
Who knows what troublous dreams may come now that I
    go to sleep?

I fear not this, but yet would live, for there is much to do,
For crime pollutes the trembling earth and murder stalks
    it through ;
My fluttering heart still leaps to think of some all-glorious
    deed,
Of oppressors to be vanquished, or of captives to be
    freed.

And since in my brief day of life, which now I know is
    past,
I did as I desire to do in this which is my last;
Over the ceasing of my works a grateful land * shall
    weep,
And its true tears shall sanctify the ground in which I
    sleep.

———

" *TÊTE D'ARMÉE.*"

(THE LAST WORDS OF NAPOLEON BUONAPARTE.)

STRETCHED on a couch the stunted "Conqueror" lies,
    Not as of yore with rich embroideries,
    Imperial purple, specked with golden bees,
But on a humble bed he, captive, dies.

The Eagle that once took its awful swoop
    Over its fields of victims, kings its prey,
    Has had of carnage its too-lengthened day,
And now is cabined in a pullet's coop.

But still the wayward mind is fluttering o'er
    The sickening quarry of its hunted things,
    Gloating o'er bleeding, weltering, festering kings,
And glutting its rank appetite with gore.

* Greece.

Worn, wasted, weak the frame, and dull the eyes,
    Languid the limbs, and scant the fevered breath ;
    The scorched-up lip is scarred, but e'en in death
Defiance takes the place of fitter sighs.

Mercy's sweet angel from the horrid bed
    With undelivered message flew at last :
    She waited long.   Her final moment passed,
And one fresh fiend sprang from a man now dead.

Th' ambitious spirit as it left its shell
    Shrieked with exulting ardour, " Tête d'Armée ! "
    One withering shout of devils' mockery,
Derisive laughter shook the vaults of hell.

" Tête d'Armée ? "   Oh no ! a mightier one ;
    SATAN, a master mind, is ruler here !
    Down to the common ranks of guilt and fear :
Thy poor ambition's past ! Low fool, thy task is done.

———

WRITTEN IN AMERICA, A.D. *1838.*

I WALK by mighty Hudson's stream,
    Tread lands beyond the Atlantic sea,
The distance is but as a dream,
    It seems my fatherland to me ;

I listening sigh, for all around
    The small birds' music fills the air;
How can I deem it foreign ground?
    Why, all my well-known flowers are here.

I look, and meet a brother's face,
    I am my kindred folk among;
I speak not to a foreign race,
    They answer in my native tongue;
I walk into the house of God,
    There they address the self-same prayer;
I view the neighbouring burial sod,
    The kindred dust commingles there.

I tread the quays, and side by side
    The States' and Island's ships are ranged;
I scan the laws, my loved Isle's pride,
    They are, except in form, unchanged;
I view their stage, and high o'er all
    Our Shakespeare fills the honoured place;
To genius kindred spirits fall;
    Can such be deemed a foreign race?

Great nation, deem us brothers then,
    And grasp the hand a land extends;
View all the world as fellow-men,
    View us as kinsmen, brothers, friends;

The same in language, manners, laws,
　　Let us in kindness pledge our troth ;
Ours surely is a common cause ;
　　Who injures one must injure both.

Our ripened institutions lend
　　To you their sanctity and name,
And, rich heir-looms, to you descend,
　　Purchased by many a deathless fame :
Drawing your origin from us,
　　And fed with such immortal food,
Born, nursed, enriched, ennobled thus,
　　What *can* ye be, but great and good ?

And should your Parent Island fall,
　　As Greece and Rome have fallen before,
May you, her GIANT CHILD, recall
　　The shade of greatness then no more,
Catch the bright spirit ere it flies,
　　Ere a dark gloom around is hurled,
Purge out its few impurities,
　　And give it perfect to the world !

NIAGARA.

To look upon Niagara !   How long
   That wish had nestled in my inmost breast !
For I had read of it in poet's song,
    And, loving Nature best when lowliest drest,
    I longed to see her in her Monarch-vest,
Her garb of homely beauty laid aside,
    Yet feared to think which I might love the best,
The lowly streamlet of the hillock's side,
Or the great foaming mass of waters in their pride.

And now I hear the distant torrent's roar
   A full, deep, rumbling and incessant sound,
Like when the ground-sea lashes England's shore,
    As if't would move the rocks which wall her round ;
    (Fit guardians of that blest, that holy ground ;)
And now a vapour-pillar points the site
    Where from its channel the vast stream must bound,
And the great river hastens from my sight
To go it knows not where ; yet powerless is its might,

On it must flow ! and not in stealthy streams,
   With pace unnoted, as it flowed of yore,
But with face ruffled to a thousand seams,
    Which pointed rocks, jagged and uneven tore,
    Struggling it passes, clinging to the shore ;

But soon, its wave-worn channel sinking low,
　　It rushes onward with impetuous roar,
Driven to the brink by its time-waging flow,
And takes its awful plunge into the gulf below.

Come, let me view the wonder ! let me look
　　On Nature, in her grandeur and her power,
Reading the fairer portions of her book,
　　I may have missed her in her solemn hour.
　　Seeking fresh beauty in each wildling flower,
And melody in every woodland song,
　　I have not seen her when her features lower,
Or known the terrors that to God belong,
Not viewing, in His might, the terrible, the strong.

Come, let me look into the great abyss ;
　　See the great rush, "the whirlwind" and "the storms ;"
Hear the vast din where oceans " howl and hiss,"
　　And fell destruction loveliness deforms.
　　Where is the horror which so much alarms,
At which alike timid and strong turn back ?
　　I hear no howls, I see no horrid forms,
Nor dream of nations', or of nature's wrack ;
I see a mighty, but a lovely cataract.

No terrors sit upon its smiling brow,
   There sunshine plays upon the waters clear,
And as it pours its mighty flood below,
   Sunshine and glory make their dwelling there.
   I wonder and admire, but cannot fear,
All is so lovely and so beautiful.
   See, the blest bow of many tints is here,
A sevenfold bow, with promised safety full,
Spanning the glorious whole, each rising fear to lull.

In floods of grandeur and of love combined,
   Here Goodness sits upon a godlike throne,
A glorious type of the Eternal Mind,
   Which tim'rous mortals fear to think upon,
   So much of majesty around is thrown,
The gazer fears to raise his eye above :
   But as the awe-struck wonderer gazes on,
The misty veil and shrinking fears remove,
Showing one glorious flood of beauty and of love.

Pour on for ever, thou almighty flood,
   Thy stream of goodness thus ; for ever flow,
Unchanging emblem of infinitude,
   Nor deem thy bounty needs a course more slow ;
   Unmeasured fountains pour their wealth below,

Where diamond wells in deep concealment lie,
   And constant streams that never ebb can know,
For ever flowing bring their rich supply,
Fed by eternal springs—springs that can never dry.

Flow on, Niagara !   For ever flow
   In power supreme, with peerless beauty bright ;
Flow thus for ever, that the world may know
      How greatness and how goodness may unite
      In beauty perfect, and unmatched in might,
Wielding eternal power with Godlike arm ;
   On thee securely rests the enraptured sight,
No shrinking dread, no fears of wrong alarm,
Thy glorious power subdues and awes us but to charm.

Still on thy rocks, capped by the mountain pine,
   May flowers of humbler growth their beauties show,
In rich festoons still hang the wildling vine,
      And the red rose and orange lily blow,
      Whilst lowlier grass and countless mosses grow
On the vast footsteps of thy giant throne,
   And, fed by dews which ever fall below,
Boast an eternal verdure all their own,
Which the enchanted sight delights to rest upon.

Pour on, Niagara, for ever pour
 Thy treasure-flood and all around thee bless ;
Thy diamond gifts in ceaseless bounty shower,
 Enriching all, and yet thy store no less ;
 Flow on, and let th' admiring world confess,
No bounds thy beauty or thy bounty knows ;
 Blest shrine, where undeluded pilgrims press,
While each an offering on thy altar throws,
 Blessing the mighty Source from which all glory flows.

———

THE SPIRIT OF THE YOUNG MAN'S HOME.

 THRICE happy Spirit, who doth preside
 Over the young man's blest fireside ;
 Who all his earthly cares beguileth,
 And round his happy circle smileth ;
 Who sitteth upon honeyed lips
 And waiteth till he comes and sips.
 SPIRIT OF LOVE, we hail thee !   Come !
 Thou Spirit of the young man's home.

 'Tis Love from baby eyes that peepeth ;
 'Tis Love with infant-joy that leapeth ;
 'Tis Love with untaught voice that singeth ;
 'Tis Love whose tiny finger clingeth ;

In every infant look and sound,
Love, all-pervading Love, is found.
SPIRIT OF LOVE, we hail thee!   Come!
Thou Spirit of the young man's home.

In summer skies, in youth's sweet morning,
In every tint those times adorning,
In every odour that perfumeth
When every flower is sweet and bloometh.
'Tis Love produceth the delight ;
'Tis Love must to the feast invite.
SPIRIT OF LOVE, we hail thee !   Come !
Thou Spirit of the young man's home.

And when a short gloom hangs before us,
'Tis but a cloud just passing o'er us ;
Each drop which falls the cloud will lighten,
And, does but help the sky to brighten.
Beyond the cloud and far above,
There ever shines the sun of Love.
SPIRIT OF LOVE, we hail thee !   Come !
Thou Spirit of the young man's home.

THE SPIRIT OF THE OLD MAN'S HOME.

" My hope is in thee."—PSALM xxxix. 7.

SPIRIT of Hope, in age's dwelling,
Of peace, of joy, of heaven telling;
Who makes the sweet hour taste the sweeter,
Who makes the fleet year pass the fleeter;
Who, as life hastens to its close,
Shows brighter things than mere repose.
SPIRIT OF HOPE, we hail thee!   Come!
Thou Spirit of the old man's home.

Without thee, what were age's thinkings,
The mind's decay, the spirit's sinkings?
The bowed-down frame, weak, aged, and shaking,
Would dread the parting soul's forsaking.
Who could withstand such years of fear,
With nought beyond the grave to cheer?
SPIRIT OF HOPE, we hail thee!   Come!
Thou Spirit of the old man's home.

Yes!   Blest with Hope, though days were sadder,
Each were a step on Jacob's ladder,

An upward step ! The rocky pillow
Again may sink in passion's billow.
Each step removes us from the ground,
Makes more distinct each heavenly sound.
SPIRIT OF HOPE, we hail thee ! Come !
Thou Spirit of the old man's home.

But there are brighter things than this ;
See, expectation's lost in bliss
And faith in sight. See, promise fadeth
In the great glory that pervadeth ;
'Mid one loud hymn of constant praise,
Through countless, never-ending days.
SPIRIT OF HOPE, we hail thee ! Come !
Thou Spirit of the old man's home.

THE DEAD MAN'S BOAT.

TO-DAY I saw a lifeless thing,
With shattered frame and drooping wing,
Now drifting here, now drifting there,
As winds or currents chanced to bear ;
Without a guiding mind or will,
It drifted onward, backward still.
" What is it," said I, " that I note ? "
" It is," said one, "the dead man's boat."

"Whose was the boat?　When was't he died?"
I asked again, and then I sighed;
For, I bethought me, when we die
How many things neglected lie!
The " trim-built wherries " that we prize
Are common boats to common eyes,
They drift about while still they float,
And each is but a dead man's boat.

"Whose was the boat?　Why, don't you know?
The boat belongs to Long-yarn Joe;
He isn't dead, but just as good—
He's like his boat, old worn-out wood;
When first he had the stomach-gout
He took the oars and rudder out,
And left it anywhere to float;
And there it is—a dead man's boat.

" Lawks! there are many here about
Belong to those who haven't gout;
I know a big old Parish Church,
That long has had the dead man's lurch,
Without one compass, rudder, sail—
A water-logged old tub or pail;
It drifts, just managing to float,
A rumbling, tumbling, dead man's boat.

5

" 'Tis sometimes full of old men's noise,
'Tis sometimes full of prating boys,
'Tis sometimes smutched with showy paints—
Whitewash makes seemly boats and saints—
And then, of course, it is pretended
That the old rotten boat is mended ;
I'll wage a sovereign to a groat,
Whitewash ne'er saved a dead man's boat."

" Don't libel thus that boat, old sinner ;
There's yet some fine old timber in her ;
Replace what time has rendered rotten
With heart of oak ; she's sound at bottom.
Caulk up her seams, make good her keel,
She'll centuries serve the public weal ;
There's not a nobler craft afloat
Than what you've called a dead man's boat.

" A stalwart crew, a manly mess,
Was granted her by good Queen Bess ;
And William afterwards supplied
What tyrants Charles and James denied.
Again she's got a leeward lurch,
But once man honestly ' The Church ; '
No British sea will ever float
With one sham flag, one dead man's boat.

MAKING BABY LINEN.

A PICTURE.

A PRETTY creature, just nineteen,
With light brown hair, and soft blue een,
Red lips, with rows of pearls between.

A form with varied charms abounding,
Where Beauty's self might sit as crowned in,
Once spare, but now a little rounding.

A neck as white as drifted snow
Its curl-hid arch now bending low ;
Long fingers, trembling while they sew.

A little square of linen white,
Almost a kerchief size—not quite—
With two small holes, one left, one right.

That little square of linen is
The shadowing of a novel bliss,
Well worth th' expectant mother's kiss.

Ah, well-a-day ! will it be worn
By something which shall soon be born,
Or will no sunshine greet that morn ?

Oh, when the fancied time arrives,
Will she, the happiest of wives,
Think the day worth a thousand lives?

Will she, amid her new alarms,
See placed in her dear husband's arms
A new-formed thing of matchless charms?

Will drooping eyes, suffused with joy,
See manly lips kiss a wee toy?
Will *his* dear voice exclaim, " My boy "?

When the small feet shall move about,
How often she will then go out !
The sun will always shine, no doubt.

And when her boy begins to talk
How pleasant then will be each walk !
Nothing shall such sweet pleasure baulk.

And when arrive his school-boy days,
And rightly he each lesson says,
How he will gain his master's praise !

And as he grows to man's estate,
With father's mind, and form, and gait,
He's sure to be both good and great.

Or if the first should be a girl,
He will find grace in every curl;
Each day will some new charm unfurl.

For if one moment of alloy
Should check the all but perfect joy,
He'll say, " All right, she'll nurse the boy ! "

Thus stitch, stitch, stitch, the fingers play,
And quickly move on, day by day,
And thought-filled hours thus fly away.

Oh, may no disappointment mar
These lovely hopes, these hopes which are
Bright as the morning's brightest star !

May fingers move and never ache,
And future shirt and chemise make,
For future little babies' sake !

And may the babies come, and prove
Each one a little " treasure trove,"
Well worthy of its parents' love !

Thus may the pleasant world move on,
A daughter now, and now a son ;
And sometimes two instead of one.

A WORD ON DEATH.

(WRITTEN ON THE DEPARTURE OF MY NIECE SUSY.)

LISTEN ! and I will speak of Death.   I have just left the
　　dead ;
Have touched the hands, have kissed the lips, whence
　　warmth and life have fled ;
Have decently laid straight the limbs, have closed the
　　fixing eye,
Have done what dearest friends must do to those whom
　　they see die.

I speak of death !   Droop not the head, and do not think
　　of pain ;
Have you e'er seen one die whom you could pray should
　　live again ?
When those we love depart from us we weep as men
　　should weep,
But who, e'en then, could ever wish to break their placid
　　sleep ?

I have seen pilgrim fathers, worn, agèd, bowed-down
　　men
Pass the last feeble moments of their threescore years
　　and ten ;

I have seen youth in beauty droop, with all the world
    could give,
And wondered at the Providence which said it should
    not live.

But all the solemn moments that I have spent beside
The beds where those I loved in life and love in death
    have died,
Have been so placid and serene, sweet ceasings of the
    breath,
Without a pain or fear, they make me quite in love with
    death.

My father and my mother dropped like some well-
    ripened fruit
With fifty or a hundred-fold of goodness at their root ;
And now, as sweet a blossom as e'er bloomed upon the
    earth
Has fallen with all its promises of purity and worth.

I pace the room (why darkened ?) and I look upon the
    bed,
And view the pale set features of the beautiful—the
    dead—
All cold, and fixed, and motionless, that smile for ever
    gone,
Which warmed to smiles and happiness all that it rested
    on.

For ever gone? That beauty, that sweetness, and that
    grace?
The virtue, purity, the heaven which beamed in that
    sweet face?
For ever lost that goodness? No! I would rather
    think
The moon, the sun, the stars above, the universe should
    sink!

'Twill live again. SHE LIVES AGAIN! E'en my beclouded
    faith
Already sees her triumphing victorious over death:
All light, all love, all innocence, her few slight faults
    forgiven,
Ranged with congenial spirits in her congenial heaven.

She lives again! I feel it now through these fast-
    dropping tears,
She lives, and I shall see her despite these doubts and
    fears;
There's not one noble thought which lights the humblest
    of the sod,
There's not one spark of virtue, but is a part of God.

POETIC SITES.

TOMB OF ROSAMOND.

THE tomb of the world's rose !   And is it here
That the fair Rosamond's sweet form was laid ?
Come, let us view it.   Now for diamond eyes
That set all hearts a-beating ; the red lips
Pressed by her king's alone ; the swan-like neck,
Hung with a nation's pearls, and not less white.
   Oh ! we shall see a smile which will enchant
Even the chilly heart of age to love,
A form which sylphs might envy, and a grace
And majesty excelling excellence.
Come, we'll remove the lid, and see for once
Embodied beauty ; for what lovely flower
Can match with the sweet " rose of all the world "?
Yet stay ! Drink not with your strained eyes too deep
A draught of beauty, nor with unchecked gaze
Let your wild spirits wander, lest the sight
Of such perfection should unfit the heart

For future bliss elsewhere—

           See, it is—there !

A crumbled pinch of dust !

           A breath—'tis gone !

Never to be collected till the winds,
And earth, and seas give back their particles
To be re-formed.   And is this beauty's boast?
A few years' reign alone, and is it gone ?
Oh ! if no virtue hallow the poor clay,
Regard not beauty.   Penitence may yield
Its evening light, but 'tis a fearful chance
For us ephemerals to lavish day
Counting on twilight.   Poor frail Rosamond,
Pity her fate and shun it.

SHAKESPEARE'S GRAVE.

IN THE CHANCEL OF HOLY TRINITY CHURCH, STRATFORD-ON-AVON.

THE dust of Shakespeare is enclosèd here,
Here, by the very altar of his God.
From hence let all " for Jesu's sake forbear
To move these bones," which in less holy place
Were bowed unto and worshipped as becomes
Not man to bow to man.   But even here
Still let us pay the highest reverence
Which we may yield to genius half divine,

Nor let the fancy rove in a wide swerve
For recollections of his wit alone.
Let us not yield to Shakespeare's mighty mind
The stinted homage a mere rhymester claims.
Delightful moralist ! with giant's grasp
He held the passions which direct mankind,
And moved them all to virtue, showing vice,
Crowned vice, torn nightly by those "terrible dreams,"
Which make e'en conquerors tremble, and meek virtue
Happy, though compassed by a prison's walls.

    Shakespeare could jest, and prudery may frown,
But must confess he ne'er laughed virtue down :
But whether grave or gay, through smile or jest,
He led the heart to Virtue and to Love.

ON VISITING " THE THIEVES' HOUSE,"

WEST STREET, SMITHFIELD, 1850.

COME, rank, and see for once how vice is bred,
Nursed, cradled, perfected among the poor ;
See how for centuries the squalid nooks
Grow up among us; adding, year by year,
Intricate way to way, till, labyrinthed
Secure at last, vice revels as it wills,
Deepens to horror and becomes sublime.

Yes, with its perfumed kerchief, oft applied,
Rank visits *now* this scenic throne of vice,
Pleased at th' excitement ! and will leave the spot
And never ask, " How much have I built up
Of this sad monument ? "

                    Legislator, come !
Come, palace-housed ! come, humbler citizen !
Come, ye neglecters of your fellow-men,
Triflers with man's great essence, who have starved
And dwindled down body and soul alike !
Come, read this bitter lesson.   Know, that man
Hath power for good or ill ; the good shows first
In the sweet buddings of the infant's smile ;
Nurtured by kindness, it to virtue grows ;
But, checked by the world's cold frost, it soon shrinks
     down,
Concentring in itself, like the gnarled oak,
Terrible power ; and when next 'tis seen,
'Tis to repay, from some such haunt as this,
The wicked world's oppression and neglect
By pillage, or the wildness of revenge.

WALTHAM CROSS.

HAIL, hallowed monument of wedded love,
That blessed remnant of the forfeit bliss
We lost with Eden.   Hail, thou solemn tribute
Of Edward to his Ellen ; sweet remembrance
Of a wife's love and husband's gratitude.
Hail, holy witness that in kingly hearts
The milder passions may predominate ;
That love indeed may nestle in a crown,
Scaring ambition thence.
                              Oh, it is sweet
To turn from history's all blood-stained leaves,
To glow o'er such a tale ; to see a queen
Participating in the kindly throbs
Which beat in humble hearts, and risking life
For her dear mate.   What more could cotters do ?
Read the bright page which hands the record down,
The sweetest tale that e'er was told of kings ;
And let each manly bosom swell with pride,
That they were monarchs of the happy isle
Whose kings are men, whose men are almost kings.
Oh happy land ! where monarchs are endowed
With human hearts ; and use their sovereignty
To guard the circle of domestic joys,
Which British kings and subjects share alike.

HOLYROOD.

A GOODLY temple to the meek-eyed goddess—
The soul-subduer, Pity.   Who e'er dreams
Of pomp, or pageantry, or princely halls,
Or royal ceremonials, by these walls ;
Who sighs for gauds, or could breathe here a wish
For the poor mockery, greatness ?

                      Sigh for her
Who, palace-housed, was yet without a home,
Twice diadem'd, who lacked the pearl content—
The priceless pearl which princes vainly seek.
Poor Mary Stuart !   Here in HOLYROOD
Was heard thy people's welcome to their queen ;
Here, too, the soul-entrancèd Rizzio drank
His draughts of love and beauty from thine eyes,
And paid his tragic penalty.   Here danced,
In gracefulness of form, the youthful Darnley,
Too soon to meet—but who delights to dwell
On such sad histories ?   Oh ! who would call
A needless tear into the eye of beauty,
Or for a well-turned period seek to move
With pain the bosoms which should rise with joy ?
Enough that here hearts high attuned for love
Sought the gay scenes of court-magnificence

For lasting happiness, and this vast palace
Yielded no joyous niche.   Alas for happiness!
'Tis not for time or place to mould it—No !

———

RUNNYMEDE.

A VISION of the past.—" I am a serf
On English ground.   Oppression's chain has bound
And galled my limbs for thirty weary years,
Which I have pined away beside the banks
Of the majestic Thames.   Oh, while it flowed
So clear, so constant, and so beautiful,
Oft have I thought how blest a people were
Unfettered by its side!   How proud a spot,
Where to a port it deepens, 'twere to build
A merchant city, a vast mural fane,
To the twin spirits, Trade and Liberty,
Thence blessings to diffuse to all the world ;
And the wide world, no ceremony else,
Would own the rite by a loud song of praise."
    A vision yet, for the serf's dream goes on :—
" The tramp of mail-clad warriors shakes the soil
Of Runnymede.   Ten thousand hands have fallen
On swords made bright and drawn for freedom's cause.
A shout of loud defiance fills the air—
A tyrant quakes, and, trembling, adds his name

To the Great Charter—one unworthy word
In the blest page of English Liberty."
The dream was prophecy.

THE BRIDGE OF SIGHS.

The Bridge of Sighs ! the narrow-vaulted passage
Which leads the doomed Venetian to the end
Of his sad life of crime !

                  And is it so ?
Sigh those o'er punishment who smile at crime ?
Mourn we, then, Guilt's detection and disgrace,
And would we see it rear its daring head,
Scorning the garb which modest Virtue wears ?
Alas ! not so.   Yet man may weep for man,
Though high the soul may swell at noble deeds,
And shrink from all dishonour; nay, though justice
May sometimes claim the extreme penalty,
And its strong hand incarnadine, forgetting
The mercy all must ask, honour may yet
Weep over the dishonoured ; we may weigh
What natural weakness, chance, or circumstance
May have subdued to guilt, and give a tear
To our fallen brother on the Bridge of Sighs.
  Cherish the whispers of the angel, Pity;

There's not one feeling of the human heart
More purifying than the seraph breath
Which Virtue sighs o'er Sin.

TOMB OF ABELARD AND ELOISE.

How wondrous the varieties of love !
With some, the stream glides on with sluggish pace,
Scarce rippling into passion ; cold and pure
Through all its course as at its virgin spring :
With some it flows as clear but more profound,
Calm though not dull, and constant though serene :
Sometimes it claims a wider range, and runs
In its full current, onward to the sea,
O'erleaping all its obstacles.   With some
It swells, a mountain torrent ; raging down
Its ravined bed it drives its ruin-course,
Whelming, destroying all in its abyss.
    Pity the unskilled mariners who dared
A wave so wide and wild.   Pity and forgive
Poor Abelard and Eloise : they lived
Their hour of wildness and romance.   Apart
They cherished in their inmost souls a love
Vain as the enthusiast's unsubstantial dreams,
Which fade with the first light.   Apart, apart,

Torn by the cold and ruthless world apart,
But not in death divided; the fair forms
Which held their beating hearts lie crumbling here,
Mingling in one dear sod; and now, perhaps,
Their spirits, reunited, aye rejoice
That they are met again.   Oh! ye young hearts,
Bear with your partings, for there is a shore
Where ye shall meet again to part no more.

KENILWORTH.

ALAS! for the high eyries of the great!
Safer the lark's nest built upon the ground;
Aye! and more beautiful; the lowly homed
Live a blest life of quietness and love,
While they who build upon an eminence
Build upon danger's brink; the lightning's flash,
The tempest's blast, nay, a mere sudden gust
May sweep to ruin.   Such Ambition's fate,
And of ambition my short story is.
    Once a fair dove, wooed by a lordly mate,
A Monarch-bird, looked with ambitious eye
Unto an eagle's nest, and sought to reach it:
She left her dove-cote, and by a bold flight
Achieved her aim, and rested by the side
Of her new mate.   The lordly mountain bird

Was daring then the sunbeam, and the dove
Dared too its gaze, and fell.

                'Tis an old tale,
The dove was Amy Robsart, and the nest
Was the proud dwelling of the princely bird
Who built up Kenilworth.

TOMB OF JULIET.

TEARS for the Mantuan pair:
To Romeo and Juliet give your tears,
Tears hot as those on Passion's burning cheek!
Sighs from each lover for the slaughtered doves;
Sighs deep as those which fan up Etna's fires!
O world, world, world! cold, false, unfeeling world,
Must all love's votaries be martyred thus?
O heartless, miser world, that wouldst not spare
Of thy wide limits but the little space
That such a pair required for life and love.

    Romeo, the young, the lover, e'en to love
Stronger than death or madness. Juliet too,
Our pretty Jule that " stinted and said aye,"
The night-masked maiden that dared tell her love,
And lived upon it till the merry lark's
Gay song seemed plaintive as the nightingale's—

Our own high-feelinged daughter of the south,
That chose her bridal in the chilly tomb
If it but gave her Romeo. Lovers, weep
Your hottest tears at this immortal shrine,
For hearts are here immured. If love, dear love,
The one pure passion of the human heart,
E'er homage claims, O Pilgrim ! pay it here
To Romeo and Juliet.

BAPTISM.

By Jordan's flowing stream
  A mighty preacher stood,
One word was all his theme
  Alike to vile and good.
Where'er the preacher went,
His cry was still, " Repent."

His church the wilderness,
  Yet all went out to see,
Expecting as they press
  A mightier far than he.
" Repent, ye stubborn band,
Heaven's kingdom is at hand.

" Prepare Emanuel's way,
  Let all His paths be straight,
Already dawns the day
  For which His people wait;
Repent, and be forgiven,
'Tis offered you from heaven.

" This Jordan as it flows
  Upon you thus I pour,

As pure as melting snows
  Descends the cleansing shower :
With water I baptize,
For water purifies.

" But there's a mightier One,
  The latchet of whose shoes
(The Great " well-pleasing " Son)
  I dare not to unloose ;
His baptism is higher,
'Tis spiritual fire.

" The cleansing symbol I
  Pour on your outward frame,
But He will vivify
  Your souls with inward flame,
Will breathe seraphic breath
Where all before was death.

" His Holy Spirit then
  Shall warm each mortal breast,
And renovated men
  Wait for their God's behest :
Ruled by His gentle sway
A world will then obey.

" No more will then be trod
  The ways of sin and hell,
But all will look to God
  And strive to serve Him well :
Baptized by Heaven above,
A Baptism of Love."

———

THE LAST SUPPER.

"Do this in remembrance of me."

HE took the bread, and breaking gave
  To each surrounding guest ;
From Judas, Satan's guilty slave,
  To John reclining on His breast.
" Do this wherever you may be ;
Break bread, and then remember Me."

He took the cup and poured the wine—
  A cup of glowing love—
The last he tasted of the vine,
  Except the holier wine above.
He took the cup, " Do this," said He,
" Let all do this, remembering Me."

The words of love were scarcely spoken,
  The cup was scarcely drained,

Ere the true bread of life was broken,
   And Calvary, the winepress, stained ;
This bread, this cup, where'er I be,
Jesus, I'll take, remembering Thee.

I'll take the bread, remembering all
   The broken bread hath done ;
It is the bidden ritual,
   And mystery the rite hath none.
The bread of life Thou art to me—
I eat the bread, remembering Thee.

I take the cup, for 'tis Thy word ;
   And as I drink the wine,
I drink, remembering Thee, my Lord,
   My Saviour, my Undoubted Vine.
Oh grant that I refreshed may be,
With sweet remembrances of Thee!

A MAIDEN'S EVENING PRAYER FOR HER LOVER.

HEAR, God of love, a maiden's prayer,
   Sovereign of earth and heaven above,
Bless all Thy creatures with Thy care,
   But chiefly bless the one I love.

And, as both promised we would bear
   Our evening thoughts of love to Thee,
Hear, God of mercy, hear the prayer
   He offers up to-night for me.

GOD'S MANNA.

I FEED upon Thy manna, Lord,
The heavenly droppings of Thy Word;
'Tis spread throughout the wilderness,
Each humble, seeking soul to bless.
May I one precious grain discover,
   'Twould fill Benoni's ample sack :
Is glory found ?   I've nothing over ;
   With but one promise I've no lack.

While morning's dews around are damp;
I go, alone, without the camp ;
Leave every worldly thought, and rove
To gather faith, and hope, and love.
With these refreshed, my soul, grown stronger,
   Travels its destined journey through ;
Weary, depressed, bowed down no longer,
   For Nebo yields my Canaan's view.

THE TRUE INCENSE.

"Let my prayer be set forth in Thy sight as the incense, and let the
lifting up of my hands be as the evening sacrifice."—PSALM cxli. 2.

O LORD, when I would worship Thee,
What offering wouldst Thou have from me?
Will slaughtered goats, or sheep, or kine
Be fitting offerings at Thy shrine?

Thy shrine?   The heaven's unmeasured space
Is Thy unbounded dwelling-place;
Each wide spread vale, each mountain height,
Is but an atom in Thy sight.

The world is Thine from pole to pole,
The circling planets as they roll;
The worlds on worlds, seen and unseen,
Which are, which will be, or have been.

I dare not offer things so cheap
As blood of kine, or goats, or sheep;
Nor censers whirl about Thy shrine—
The fragrance of all flowers is Thine.

Material things I dare not bring
To my eternal Spirit King;
The best and fairest of the sod
I dare not offer to my God.

But praise and prayer, and truth and love,
Are worthy offerings for above ;
If faithful, they will please Thee well ;
Not angels' songs will them excel.

Lord, at Thy feet I lowly bow,
Praise, prayer, truth, love, I offer now :
Accept these offerings, Lord, from me ;
My Father, I would worship Thee.

PSALM LXXXIV.

How blessèd, Lord, is Thy abode !
My soul longs for the house of God ;
There would my heart and flesh rejoice,
And constant praise employ my voice.

Where timorous swallows build their nest,
My peaceful spirit flies for rest,
Would learn its lessons from the dove, -
And on Thy altar offer love.

Far better than sin's thousand days
Is one short hour of prayer and praise ;
In God's blest house the humblest things
Excel the pride and pomp of kings.

My King, my God, compared with Thee,
The world is lightest vanity:
Thy service, Lord, I would fulfil,
Would sing Thy praise, would do Thy will.

CONSTANT PRAYER.

A THOUGHT on God when day begins,
Guards from a hundred thousand sins;
A thought on God ere daylight sets,
Will help to pay our unpaid debts.

A prayer, as fades each lessening hill,
Secures His care to guard us still;
Our midnight praise, unwearied yet,
Is heard, and guards of angels set.

Since constant thoughts, and praise and prayer
Secure for us Almighty care,
Oh, be our lives one constant hymn
Of praise, or prayer, or thought on Him!

THAT WHICH IS GIVEN, GIVE.

THAT which is given, give !
  That which God lends you, lend !
Those who live by you, let them live !
  Be to each friend, a friend.

All have not gold to give,
  But all may yet be kind :
Whoe'er you are, where'er you live,
  Give love to all mankind.

WOMAN'S WORKS.

LOOK round the moving world and scan
The great, the vaunted works of man ;
Huge piles of stone which seem to say,
" We dare the progress of decay ; "
But ere is placed the topmost stone,
Decay has claimed it for its own.

The vessel ploughs with venturous sweep
The furrows of the billowy deep,
And rides with monarch flag unfurled,
The proud encircler of the world ;
But tempest-moved, the mightier wave,
No more its throne, becomes its grave.

The river's bed, the mountain's mine,
Where heaps of golden treasures shine,
Are bared by man.　The glittering ore
Is added to his ample store,
But unenjoying the huge heap,
He dies and knows not who will reap.

Man toils, and on his weary face
The tears of care leave their sad trace,
As down his pallid cheek they flow,
And tell of trouble, want, and woe.
Man toils for nought, his work is vain,
Pain-bought, it purchases but pain.

But cheerful woman, far more wise,
Catches the moment as it flies,
In cloudiest hour perceives the sun,
Blest when a single smile is won;
Extracts from even night a ray,
And smiles the darkness into day.

How slight the seed from which there comes
The happy harvest of our homes !
A cheering word and sorrow flies,
A smile, and lo ! farewell to sighs :
Affection's lips no sooner move
Than reigns supreme Domestic Love.

From what pure spring is it that flows
So calm a current of repose?
Whose voice can thus at its sweet will
Say to all tumult, " Peace ! be still " ?
Whose presence sheds its light around,
And makes each fireside holy ground?

Woman's sweet influence alone
Builds in each humble cot Love's throne ;
She bids us hold as meaner things
The pride of wealth, the power of kings,
Says, " High-grown fruit is not so sweet
As the blest manna at our feet."

Oh, would we but be wise and hear
The wisdom of the Woman-Seer,
How full of joy, how bright, how blest,
Were then the world ! a world of rest—
A world where every pulse would move
To perfect bliss and perfect love.

EPITAPH.

How often death the feeble spares
    While he subdues the strong ;
And leaves the aged to their cares,
    While he removes the young !

A warning voice thus speaks to all
   Who hitherto are spared ;
None can avoid death's solemn call—
   " Let none be unprepared."

EPITAPH.

DEATH to the wicked comes with barbèd dart,
   With all the weapons of destruction armed ;
The grisly phantom frights the strongest heart,
   The boldest sinner well may be alarmed.

Death to the righteous comes with friendly voice,
   And leads but to the mansions of the blest ;
He bids the feeble, mourning soul rejoice,
   He bids the weary come and be at rest.

EPITAPH ON AN INFANT.

I SAW at morn a lovely flower,
   Which shed the sweetest perfume round ;
But ere it reached the noonday hour
   It lay, a wreck upon the ground.

And this is beauty's fate, I said,
   No mortal power its charms can save ;
For flowers will prematurely fade,
   And loveliness thus find a grave.

But 'twixt the infant and the flower,
   How vast—how blest a difference lies!
The blossom passes with its hour,
   The waking infant never dies.

CONSOLATION.

THERE is a smile for every sigh,
   For every wound a balm,
A joy for every moistened eye,
   For every storm a calm.

Each sigh is sent a smile to light,
   Each wound in mercy given,
Each moistened eye will yet be bright,
   Each storm subside in Heaven!

THE THREE CHERRIES.

" Well, sir, I am not yet so overblown,
*   But I may hang some time upon the tree,*
*   And still be worth the picking."*—TOBIN.

ON a tree, a little tree,
Once were little cherries three;
Just had fallen the fading blossoms,
And exposed their swelling bosoms:
Pretty, pretty little tree,
Pretty little cherries three.

7

As I viewed the Loves one morning,
With a blush their cheeks adorning,
Just as peeped the faintest streak
Fancy heard a cherry speak :
"I am ripened beauty's type,
Please to pick me, I am ripe."

Soon I picked the little cherry,
But unripened was the berry;
I ne'er touched my cautious lip
Even with this cherry's tip,
But 'twas flung away untasted—
Pity that it thus was wasted.

To the little tree returning,
Softened by seven noon suns' burning,
Brightly glowed the ruddy pair
I had left to ripen there;
One, as then my pleased lip felt it
In delicious sweetness melted.

Summer's sun had long been shining,
And the autumn's tendrils twining,
When I sought again the tree
For the ripest of the three :
But the cherry, long forgotten,
On its shrivelled stem was rotten.

Listen, maidens; may not cherries
Lessons give as well as fairies?
Don't then, pray, accept an offer
Solely as the maiden proffer;
But, the first temptation past,
Mind you DON'T REJECT THE LAST.

— —

CHILDREN'S SHOPS.

OUTSIDE my garden door to-day,
  On a broad step just at the top,
Some little things, in their sweet play,
  Had formed and left a "Children's Shop."

Small bits of sticks, and pipes, and straws,
  And polished pebbles of all hues,
And nut-brown hips, and scarlet haws,
  And scraps that but a child amuse.

All these were spread in best array,
  As full-grown chapmen spread their wares;
And here, no doubt, in childish play,
  Were learnt trade's lessons unawares.

A pebble with a certain spot
  Would purchase a less valued row,
And some rare crooked stick, when got,
  Would buy some settled length of straw.

7 *

A pinch of shrivelled leaves (best tea),
 Some rotten wood (an ounce of snuff);
Miss A. sold " so sheap " to Miss B.,
 " Two paper sillins,"—" twite enough."

And here they seem to come each day
 And chatter their small bargains o'er ;
Still bartering this for that in play,
 Each morning at my garden-door.

And as I passed their shop to-day,
 Hastening to reach my larger store ;
Thought I, my work is like their play,
 Egad, 'tis very little more.

We trifles make and trifles sell,
 And get but trifles for our pains ;
At the play's end 'tis hard to tell
 The object of our petty gains.

From day to day awhile we strive,
 And then, tired out, at last we stop ;
Such trifles charm us while we live,
 Ours is at best "a Children's Shop."

THE YOUNG WORKMAN.

(AN IMITATION WITH ALTERATION.)

In a chamber next the sky,
  On a narrow and low stump bed,
Lay a little fellow, four feet high,
  Resting his curly head;
His breathing was mild and sweet,
  For in health he was perfectly well,
But he started up and sprang to his feet
  At the sound of a factory bell.

"Oh! it surely can't be so,
  It isn't already five;
O lawk," said he, "here's a pretty go!
  I must dress if I wish to thrive;
My eyelids seem to sink,
  As if I could lie till seven,
What joy I should think another wink,
  And another hour's sleep would be heaven."

Ding, ding, ding, ╻
  Went the factory bell again,
The boy rubbed his eyes, and looked out on the skies
  Through his well cleaned window-pane;

A labourer bold and strong,
  Went by with the tools of his trade,
He sang aloud the well-known song,
  The song of the mattock and spade.

" Work, work, work,
  'Tis the duty and pleasure of life ;
Work steadily, work
  For yourself, and your children, and wife ;
The man who will heartily work,
  To his feet can boldly spring,
He need not wince at the frown of a prince,
  Or cringe for the smile of a king.

" Work with your right hand or left,
  Work with your shoulders or feet,
Work with your head, if a good one, instead,
  But work without any deceit.
Work, work, work
  For yourself, and your children, and wife ;
Work steadily, work,
  'Tis the duty and pleasure of life.

" To buy with the first saved pound
  Of your well-earned honest wage,
Some long-wished comforts to surround
  The wife of your youth and age ;

Chair and table and bed,
    Bed and table and chair;
On every one her smile is shed,
    And your work's reward is there.

" If one of a lowly band,
    Skilled artisan or clown,
If one of the lofty of the land,
    If the wearer of a crown,
Work honestly, work,
    Each has his taskwork given;
Work, work, work,
    'Tis the high command of Heaven :

" Full six days shalt thou work,
    And all thy labour do,
Let the seventh be given to God in Heaven,
    Who six days worked for you.
The man who will faithfully work,
    May upward cast his eye ;
For if he lacked bread, the ravens which fed
    Elijah would bring supply."

In the chamber next the sky,
    Near his narrow, low stump bed,
Stood the little fellow, four feet high,
    As he combed his curly head,

And he said, " It is all very well
  To rest till the clock strikes five,
But before the last sound of the factory bell
  I'll to work, for I wish to thrive ! "

———

THE COTTAGE OF CONTENT.

I WENT to Chelmsford yesterday,
  And though I drove eight miles the hour,
I spied a cottage on my way,
  Which I had noticed once before.

And labelled on it, black on white,
  I plainly read as past I went,
(The writer was a happy wight,)
  " This is the Cottage of Content."

So it might be.   Its walls were rough
  Slap-dashed, with lime-wash whitened o'er,
The door was made of homely stuff,
  But shut and opened !   'Twas a door.

The cottage had a garden too,
  With beds for cabbage, beans, and peas,
Fruit trees and flowers it had a few,
  And just a hive or two of bees.

The chimney smoked—so there was fire !
 Food, lodging, were each side the door.
What more could any man require ?
 With these one hardly could be poor.

" Well, really," thought I, as I leant
 Back in my chaise, and gave it speech,
" To me this Cottage of Content
 Does quite a little sermon preach."

Its happy tenant worked, no doubt,
 And had his livelihood to seek ;
He earned, by constant toiling out,
 At most eight shillings in the week ;

And was content ?   Well, so he might !
 Let's see : rent, *three pound ten*, and then
Rates, taxes, *one; two*, fire and light,
 Bread, *six ;* meat, *four*— £16 10.

Clothes, say *two pounds ;* drink, physic, *nil*,
 Books, sundries, *one;* no debts, no qualms ;
No fees or time for being ill,
 And just *ten shillings* left for alms !

Why what a stock of worldly lore
 Is in those two black lines of paint
A mine of wealth is counted o'er
 In this same Cottage of Content.

For there I read in language clear
  How each of us may live in plenty,
Just earn a full score pounds a year,
  And learn to live within the twenty.

THE PLOUGHMAN AND THE LARK.*

Sweet lark ! As breaks the day
  To each it labour bringeth,
From morn to eve I plough,
  The lark the long while singeth.

It is for me and thee
  I give the land its dressing,
God prosper thee, sweet bird,
  Ask thou for me a blessing.

* This is almost literally rendered from a prose translation of a Polish song.

FLOWERS.

THE PRIMROSE.

HAIL, lovely visitant ! The Spring's first rose,
Not warm with blushes like the deep-dyed flowers
Of summer days ; but pale as the first hope
    Of trembling early love,

When first it seeks return. While, primrose-like,
It opes its blossoms at the Spring's first smile,
Daring to death the possible return
    Of chilly Winter's time.

Alas ! the lover and the flow'ret die
Of coldness oft. Sweet Genii of the Spring,
Guardians alike of earth's and the heart's blossoms,
    Shield and protect them both.

Hold back the temptings of the sunny smiles
Which warm to unfolding the young primroses,
Till settled terms of sunshine have prepared
    All for their dear reception.

THE DAISY.

BEAUTIFUL always, ever blossoming,
　Constant as is the dear enlivening ray
Which steals upon us in the "freshe morninge,"
　When it awakes and opes the eye of day,
Lovely throughout the year, throughout all years,
Whether in the Spring's smile or Winter's tears.

Unfading, never absent little flowers,
　Not planted here and there with sparing hand,
But scattered freely, so that the bent mowers
　May sweep their scythes nor fear to rob the land.
Ten thousand fall, when drops the latter rain,
And lo ! ten thousand blossoming again.

Beautiful deckers of the skylark's nest,
　Bending o'er each young bird a mimic ray
Of the blest sun, swelling its unfledged breast
　With dreams of heavenly beauty and of day,
Teaching the tiny warblers where to sing,
When a few weeks have strengthened each small wing.

Delightful Daisy, flow'ret of my youth,
　Thou bringest me sweet dreams of early joy,
Of unsuspected, unsuspecting truth,
　Of all that the man sighs for of the boy;

Thou tellest me of those dear happy hours
When all was beautiful as thine own flowers.

O, my sweet gem, my weary bosom sighs
   To tread the footsteps of my youth anew;
To fix my upturned gaze upon the skies,
   While clinging to my native sod like you;
Oh bear me to the daisy-studded vales
I loved in youth, my sinking spirit fails!

WALLFLOWER.

   Not in the halls
Of men, when garnished is the festal board,
And flushed with pride, the castle's mighty lord
   Looks on his festooned walls.

   Not in the bower,
The flower-decked bower of love, Cheiranthus grows;
Nothing so humble there. 'Tis for the rose,
   Not for the poor Wallflower.

   Not in the spot
Where the trim gardener plants his favoured flowers,
To be admired a few short sunny hours,
   And then to be forgot.

No, lovely flower,
Thy blossoms smile where show has passed away,
Breathing their balmy fragrance o'er decay,
Cheering misfortune's hour.

In pomp unseen,
Recluse, thou stayest from the giddy throng,
An absentee from revel and from song,
Shunning the gaudy scene.

But thou giv'st bloom
To the poor falling tower and ruined wall,
And in the roofless and deserted hall,
Thou breathest thy perfume.

Like a true friend,
No smiling flatterer in a prosperous day,
But cheering and consoling when decay
Tells of vain pleasure's end.

Go whisper, then,
Sweet Wallflower, in each sigh of thy rich breath,
That Friendship's flower blooms o'er decay and death:
Go, whisper it to men!

TULIP.

IF rainbow tints or gracefulness of form
Could chain the sun-blast or resist the storm,
Or if the crowds which hang on Beauty's neck
Were fond and faithful after Beauty's wreck,
Queen of the flowers, gay Tulip, thou shouldst be,
And all would bow to beauty and to thee ;
But since, when past thy little day of bloom,
Thy fading beauty leaves us no perfume,
We dare not bow before thy beauty's shrine,
Or worship charms which fade so fast as thine.
Ah, no ! The beauty which leaves not behind
Some lasting charm, some loveliness of mind,
Some perfume of the soul which will live on
When grace of form and rainbow hues are gone,
May for a day our admiration move,
May please our fancy but not gain our love.

LILY OF THE VALLEY.

OH ! what a lovely moral tells
The Lily with its silver bells !
 Tis said they ring on summer nights,
Summoning all the fairy sprites
To meet their tiny King and Queen
Under the oak or on the green :
If so, it surely is to bless,
For how could Lily-bells do less?
Low in the vale retired it lies,
Shunning the gaze of vagrant eyes,
Close to its own dear parent earth
It clings, the type of modest worth,
But, hidden though in hood of green,
Too beautiful to be unseen,
Oft is it sought by those who prize
The modesty which fools despise,
Oft is it found by the fond few
Who can esteem its virgin hue,
And leave the flowers of gaudier dye
O'er the sweet VALLEY-FLOWER to sigh.
Oh ! is not this a happier state
Than one short hour of pride elate,

Than one bright gaudy, sunny day,
In blue and scarlet,—and away?
Some may admire, but few can prize,
The flaunting flowers of many dyes;
But I will seek the gentle one
Which seems the general gaze to shun,
Nor breathes its sigh of fragrance sweet
But to her lover at her feet.
Maidens, scorn not this humble tale
Of the sweet Lily of the Vale.

FORGET-ME-NOT.

DEAR flower, thou owest half thy fame
To the sweet magic of thy name.
How do we all delight to dwell
  On the fond hope that those we leave,
Those who have loved us long and well,
Will linger o'er our last farewell,
  And for our absence fondly grieve!
Yes! each loved spot, and tree, and flower,
Will hear them at the accustomed hour
Sighing for those who used to share
The pleasures now but shadowed there.

8

Oh, Memory ! dear charm, which binds,
In lasting fondness, kindred minds ;
Whatever fate may have in store,
    Be mine a proud or humble lot,
Content, I ask or wish no more,
    If those I love " FORGET ME NOT."

MIGNONETTE.

ALL-FRAGRANT Mignonette,
Where is thy honey-bearing blossom sighing
Its fragrance out?   'Tis all around me flying,
Though I have searchèd long without once spying
    Thy little spice-flower yet.

    Ah ! darling, thou art seen.
Oh ! strange ; and does this load of honey-sweetness,
With which the air is fillèd to repleteness,
Come from a plant, whose highest boast is neatness—
    A little tuft of green ?

    Though scarcely more than weed
Thou art in form, yet never have I, surely,
Loved any bush, or tree, or flower so purely ;
Thy fragrance wins me to thee most securely,
    My Mignonette indeed.

Flowers of each form and dye,
Even from early youth have I been wreathing,
Each to be sweet and beautiful believing,
But in return for thy sweet blossom's breathing,
    I give my heart's first sigh.

HEART'S-EASE.

In youth I planted a sweet flower
Beside my own dear infant bower ;
Its first blest buddings, all were noted,
For on my little gem I doted.
'Twas not a gay or gaudy blossom
Which gladdened thus my infant bosom ;
No flaunting flower the proud to please,
'Twas but the violet flower, Heart's-ease.
I loved it on from youth to age,
It did my every thought engage ;
Each day to tend my charge I flew,
And, with attention, it so grew,
So well repaid my anxious care,
I had enough and had to spare.
Sweet reader, may I ask if you
Would have a stock of Heart's-ease too ?
List to the moral of the sage,
" Plant it in youth, 'twill last to age."

SWEET PEA.

My little fragile favourite, whither art thou tending?
Where are now thy pliant little tendrils wending?
Thy butterfly-like blossoms, why thus are they sporting.
Whither are they wandering, or what are they courting?
I have seen roses bloom, I too have seen lilies,
Primroses and cowslips, pinks and daffodillies;
Some excel in beauty, some excel in meekness,
Little flower, I think thy charm is in thy weakness.

Even from thy birth, of flowers or plants the weakest,
Long ere thy blossoms burst, a firm support thou seekest;
And as around thy prop thou thy small tendrils wreathest,
Oh! all the sweetness there of thy fragrant soul thou
     breathest.
Sweet breath, sweet flower, sweet weakness ever clinging
To the one chosen prop from the beginning;
Oh! surely Love is here! and, tho' shadowed but in
     flowers,
Each breath, each slightest tint of the "all-beautiful" is
     ours.

GERANIUM.

How oft, from distant flower to flower,
   Like vagrant butterflies we roam,
In search of happiness each hour,
Visiting every distant bower,
   Yet never seeking it at home.

Yet, there a flower of sweetest hue,
   Has grown beneath our early care;
Its scent and beauty known to few,
Within our home its first shoot grew,
   And it has ever blossomed there.

Surely its perfume has not cloyed
   The sated or perverted sense,
Yet was its scent in youth enjoyed,
Though newer objects have decoyed
   Our wandering attentions thence.

Perhaps the summer shows us flowers,
   The sweet Geranium's tints to dim;
But soon will pass the sunny hours,
And but a wreck will then be ours
   Of all that charms our vagrant whim.

Sigh not for gay and distant things,
  For gaudy flowers no longer rove ;
They fly away on swallows' wings,
While ever in our cottage springs
  The flower of pure " domestic love."

FUCHSIA.

BESIDE the rosy bower of Love,
  Blest with the smile of sunny skies,
With sweets around it and above,
  The drooping Fuchsia poured its sighs.

For the gay Summer time had past,
  And brought no blossoms to its bough,
While Autumn plucked with envious haste
  The fading flow'rets from his brow.

Oh ! will the waning year pass by,
  Scattering on all around me bloom,
While I, unblest, unfavoured, die,
  No blush, no beauty, no perfume ?

While ever-bounteous Nature pours
  Its rainbow loveliness around,
And e'en the wreck of summer flowers
  Strews with gay beauty the rich ground ;

Must I, poor unimpassioned flower,
   Thus coldly live and nun-like die,
Growing by Love's own rosy bower
   Without one glance from his dear eye ?

Just then flew by the wayward child,
   As thus the drooping Fuchsia mourned,
And the capricious urchin smiled,
   And to the plant his arrow turned.

The bolt had scarcely left his bow,
   Ere pendant pearls from each branch move,
Which, turned to his own tint, are now
   The emblems of " accepted love."

BUTTERCUP.

THERE is an unassuming mound
   O'er which I lately sighed,
A step above the common ground,
But hidden by tall tombstones round,
   Those lettered scrolls of pride.

This mound I planted with sweet flowers
   Of every form and hue ;
Transplanted from the garden bowers,
Which saw my Ellen's happy hours,
   When I was happy too ;

The rose, the lily, the heart's-ease,
  And all the flowers she loved ;
The daisy, mignonette, sweet peas ;
Alas ! I robbed the village bees,
  And had them all removed.

I paced wherever we had trod,
  Collecting all she praised ;
With tears unknown to all but God,
I planted them within the sod
  Over her body raised.

I watched them all, yes, day by day,
  But soon each plant was gone,
For every night did some decay,
Till all were faded quite away,
  Except the humblest one.

But still a Buttercup was there
  To cheer me in my sighs,
And that to me, her worshipper,
One day seemed, *looking up to her*,
  My Ellen in the skies.

Checked was my woe, and shamed my grief
  As I the moral drew ;
It gave my sinking heart relief,
I felt our parting would be brief,
  And I looked upward too.

IRIS.

WELCOME, gay Iris, flower of many dyes,
'Twin sister of the Iris of the skies,
Bright flower-de-luce, fair bud of life and light,
Hope's own dear flower, sweet promise of delight ;
Strange that the tints of heaven's aërial bow
Should be reflected as a flower below.
But so it is.   Hope's tints are everywhere,
That man may shun the danger of despair.
True, the poor Iris of the earth is pale,
E'en the moon's rainbow tints too often fail ;
But a bright bow of mercy and of love
Spans the wide heaven, if we but look above.
How sunny bright the bow of Hope appears,
When the sky weeps its penitential tears !
Bound to my heart, dear Iris, ever be,
Blest shadow of the tints I long to see :
Why o'er each little trouble should I sigh,
When the consoler, Hope, is ever nigh ?
What, though the skies may lower and clouds may frown,
Be not, my drooping spirit, thus cast down ;
Still are there whispers of eternal rest,
Hope shadows still the pleasures of the blest,
And every hue that cheers the failing sight
Is but a fraction of eternal light.

Come to my drooping heart, immortal flower ;
Cheer and console me in misfortune's hour ;
Point to the brighter Iris of the sky.
Strong in that hope, no longer can I sigh,
I mount, I triumph, even as I die.

———

HEATH.

THE Heath, the beautiful purple Heath,
   With its blessèd brown stem ; oh ! I know it well,
With its gorse above, and its moss beneath.
There is not a flower like the purple Heath,
   It bears, and it ever shall bear, the bell.

The garden has its queen-like rose,
   But the lady demands never-ceasing care ;
Whilst the wildling Heath on each bleak spot grows,
It makes the barren moors smile where it blows,
   And freshens the breath of the upland air.

Garden flowers are for my lady's hand,
   And each fresh one adds to a plenteous store,
But the wild Heath takes a nobler stand,
It grows on the unenclosèd land,
   And blooms for the common's lords, THE POOR.

I love the Heath, and so does the bee,
  We both sip its sweets without asking leave ;
I love the Heath, for it seems to me
The very own flower of liberty ;
  And that's why I worship it morn and eve.

The Heath ! How the beautiful wild bush blows !
  The flower with the purple drops for me !
The heather tells how freedom grows,
And its emblem tint in its blossoms shows,
  The purple Heath is the flower of the free.

———

HONEYSUCKLE.

By rustic seat or garden bower,
There's not a leaf, a shrub, or flower,
Blossom or bush, excelling thee,
Lowly but fragrant honey-tree.
By stately halls we see thee not,
But find thee near the lowly cot,
On latticed porch, by humble door,
Thou leanest with thy honey store,
Dropping, from thy bee-bosomed flowers,
Sweetness through evening's dewy hours.

Tree of the cottage and the poor,
Can palace of the rich have more?
No; for content as seldom dwells
In palaces as lowly cells.
Oh, I would scorn the mansion fair,
If pomp and pride and care were there,
And to the humbler cottage flee,
Leaving each proud and lofty tree,
For thee, dear Honeysuckle, thee!

SUNFLOWER.

Flower of the morning sun,
Thy worship is begun;
  To bless thy anxious and impassioned gaze
Thy radiant god appears,
To dry up all thy tears
  With the first glance of his refulgent rays.

Flower of the noonday, turn
To where his beauties burn
  In splendour and in light, enthronèd high;
He from his throne of gold
Thy service doth behold,
  And smiling blesseth from meridian sky.

Flower of the evening sun,
Thy task of love is done,
　　Farewell ! a last farewell to all thy sorrow ;
Constant throughout thy day,
Thy god with parting ray
　　Promised to smile again on thee to-morrow.

———

HYDRANGEA

"The beautiful blossoms of the Hydrangea are not its flowers, but Bractea, or floral leaves. They possess few of the regular organs of the flower, and could produce neither fruit nor seed."

I OFTEN pass a leisure hour
　　Within a neighbour's garden grounds,
And there is scarcely shrub or flower
　　But I have noticed in my rounds ;
And all I see I love, but one
Which I have marked, and marked to shun.

I saw its bursting blossoms rise,
　　Of greenish white, or sickly blue ;
But soon it wooed the sunny skies,
　　And robbed them of their roseate hue,
And with a rose's beauty spread
The bunchèd honour of its head.

And whilst it blossomed thus its hour,
 I saw the young and idle gaze,
They viewed the false one as a flower,
 And on it lavished their vain praise ;
Whilst them it pleases, me it grieves;
Alas ! its blossoms are but leaves.

They please the uninstructed eye,
 And charm perhaps awhile the vain,
But soon the rosy leaves will die,
 And neither fruit nor seed remain.
How can I then but thus despise,
Since all is gone when beauty dies !

———

SNOWDROP.

WHO knows not the pale virgin flower
Of winter's wild and chilly hour?
When trees are bare and sunbeams fled,
It rises from its icy bed ;
Not warm with blushes like the rose,
But white as its own parent snows.
With drooping head and timid eye
Averted from the passer-by,

It woos no love, it seeks no praise,
Like the rich flowers of sunnier days ;
But heralding the coming spring,
The SNOWDROP, pure and guileless thing,
Shadows the pleasures which are ours,
In childhood's unimpassioned hours,
Ere yet the heart has learnt to sigh
For long-sought, unfound sympathy,
While the bright day has brought no night
To chill, to wither, and to blight.
   Oh, 'tis delightful to recall
The few sweet moments (sweet to all),
The blessèd springtime of our youth,
When all was innocence and truth ;
And if we only could retain
A lesson so refined and plain,
   How lengthened out to age would be
Our angel hours of purity !

DYING ROSES.

SIGH for the rose, yes, even for a rose ;
   I would not that one lovely thing should die :
So beautiful is every flower which blows,
   I cannot see one fading, and not sigh.

Not one frail bloom upon the grassy hills
　　But does its part to purify the breeze ;
The healing balsam which the welkin fills,
　　Oozes from blossoms as minute as these.

Then sigh not for the rose—not for the rose :
　　Its blooming past, its leaves and petals die ;
But on the breeze its fragrant essence flows,
　　A sweet for ever on the perfumed sky.

———

A BIRTHDAY TRIBUTE TO MY SISTER.

Long has my harp, dear sister, hung
　　Upon the willow bough ;
　　Had not its chords affection strung,
Perhaps it still had noiseless swung
　　To winter breezes now.

Dear girl, our hearts were always one,
　　Even in childhood's hours,
And union blesses still our home,
As when you know we used to roam
　　And twine our gathered flowers.

Well, we can think without a sigh
   Upon our youthful years ;
For in the happy days gone by
We have not wet affection's eye,
   Except with pleasure's tears.

Mem'ry is sweet to those who live
   As if their lives would last ;
And, sister, could I now receive
The brightest pleasures hope can give,
   I would not yield the past.

How could I part with every thought
   On which I love to dwell ?
With such sweet pleasures are they fraught,
That happiness were dearly bought
   In bidding them farewell.

The smiles of youth, and oh, its tears—
   Its very tears are sweet ;
Affection still each look reveres,
And every word that love endears,
   'Tis luxury to repeat.

Do you forget, when full of play,
   We toddled down the hill,
What moralising friends would say ?
Yet many years have passed away,
   And we are happy still.

Time smiled upon our youthful hours,
  They glided swiftly by;
But still he strews our path with flowers,
He sears indeed our birthday bowers,
  But with the softest sigh.

And as the future years pass on,
  If care our bliss alloys,
We'll snatch the pleasures ere they're gone,
Forget the sorrows one by one,
  And only keep the joys.

Each coming year will surely bring
  Some beauty to the mind;
And as young folly takes its wing,
We'll keep the blossoms of our spring,
  And leave its thorns behind.

We'll keep, without the froward tears,
  The innocence of youth;
Simplicity, without its fears,
The caution of our riper years,
  With all our childhood's truth.

And let us hope that future years
  Will smile as have the past;
We have had much that life endears,
And hope as bright a promise bears,
  That happiness will last.

Of the dark threatening cloud of care,
  Less cheerful lips may tell;
Most have of happiness their share,
Their days of sunshine in the year,
  If they but prize them well.

And though our spring-time has not worn
  Ne'er-changing, cloudless skies,
We still have had some sunny morns,
Roses have mingled with our thorns,
  And pleasures with our sighs.

What could we ask?   I have seen those
  Whose lot has been as mild,
Sink under their ideal woes,
While we have borne the little blows
  Of fortune, and have smiled.

Still let us smile.   A few more years,
  At most a very few;
A few more hopes, a few more fears,
A few more days of smiles and tears,
  We bid this world adieu.

A FATHER'S LOVE.

DEAR one, ere yet upon thy baby brow
    The first faint dawnings of thy mind appeared,
I loved thee for thy own dear self; and now,
    When love repays my love, oh, how endeared,
How almost idolized, my child, art thou!
May no rude wind shake from the lovely bough
    The pure and fragrant blossoms of thy spring,
Oh! may the great All-merciful allow
    Nothing to stain my pure and spotless thing!
    May every rising sun some bounty fling
On thy fair cheek, my pretty opening flower,
    The pure and virgin white envermeiling
With each warm tint; but yet from beauty's bower
Withhold each blush.   My child, be purity thy dower.

A MOTHER'S LOVE.

FROM the close-textured and deep-rooted trees
    Proceed the light and sylph-like blossoming things,
Which the bright jocund eye delighted sees,
    Decking the boughs in our sunshiny springs,
Gladdening the little honeysucking bees,
    When they first see the peach-bloom's ruby rings
Marrying the young sunshine and the breeze.

As light, as delicately touched as these,
    Art thou, my beautiful child ; and yet I trace,
Though writ in softest lines (oh ! how they please),
    The manly vigour of thy father's face !
He sees it too ; watches thee on my knees,
And says each day adds to thy form a grace.
O God, my grateful heart's too big for its small space.

A BROTHER'S LOVE.

Twin branch, that with me budded, blossomed, grew,
    Each intertwined with each ; decking the bower
Of love, our home.   Sweet sister, how on you
    Has each fond thought rested since childhood's hour !
    Noting the deepening tints, as my sweet flower
Blushed into beauty.   First the rose's hue
    Glowed on your healthful cheek, a priceless dower ;
Then Love his tremulous tint of purest blue
    Shed from your eyes.   Unconscious of its power,
You then unwittingly its glances threw
    Upon a passing stripling.   Happy hour,
If with its power of beauty, he then knew
    The all-enduring fragrance of the flower,
    He then had made his home an amaranthine bower.

GRANDFATHER GREY AND GRAND-
DAUGHTER GAY.

Oh, tell me, my dear little schoolfellow, pray,
If ever you saw my old Grandfather Grey;
His face is so wrinkled, his eyes are so dim,
Yet I never can think without pleasure on him.
He kisses and calls me his Granddaughter Gay;
You don't know how I love my dear Grandfather Grey.

How funny he looks when he munches his bread,
He scarcely has got a tooth left in his head;
But since he can't eat the least bit of the crust,
He must have the crumb—don't you think, dear, he must?
And the teeth which he praises of Granddaughter Gay
Shall eat up the crusts for her Grandfather Grey.

And though he can walk yet, and says he is hale,
He tells me that shortly his old legs will fail,
That his steps will soon cease to be nimble and quick
(Already he asks me to bring him his stick).
If assistance he wants, here's his "dear little Gay"
Will be a support to her "Grandfather Grey."

I'll hem all his kerchiefs, the red and the blue;
O dear, how I wish I knew something to do!

He speaks and he does all so kindly to me,
And I've nothing by which all my love he can see;
But I know that he loves his dear pet, little Gay.
And he knows that I love my dear Grandfather Grey.

THE WILD ANEMONÉ.

In some fair grounds in Charlton road
    I strolled with Prue to-day,
And at one moment we both saw
    A wild Anemoné.

We looked into each other's eyes,
    And they were wet with tears;
We almost heard each other's sighs,
    Both travelled back ten years.

Ten years ago—the March was mild—
    Ten years this very day,
In Hornsey Wood, a darling child
    Plucked an Anemoné.

With joyous care she brought it home,
    As a stray precious thing;
She did not know what loveliness
    God scatters every spring.

I told the little which I knew
  Of Nature's lovely blooms ;
I spoke of each wild blossom's hue,
  And of their sweet perfumes.

How every hillock had its flower,
  Which man might never see ;
How some might bloom but one short hour,
  To feed one honey-bee.

But though thus scattered everywhere,
  O'er hill, and vale, and plain,
No scent was wasted in the air,
  No beauty bloomed in vain.

Sometimes it pleased a sated sense,
  While wafted on the wind;
Sometimes a flower's more rich incense
  Made holier a mind.

Like angel flowers, for earth too fair,
  Which, ripened for above,
Had still a happy mission here,
  And shed their seeds of love.

Our darling smiled, she faintly smiled,
  And gave a silent kiss ;
She was herself (the precious child)
  Full ripened then for bliss.

And scarcely had the flower decayed,
    (That wild Anemoné)
Before that pure and gracious maid
    Had from us passed away.

But each sweet look, and smile, and sigh
    Drops on us all around :
Oh, scattered goodness cannot die,
    Even in thorny ground !

ON THE RECOVERY OF A YOUNG LADY FROM ILLNESS.

WHEN beauty droops we mourn its sigh,
    But ne'er expect its young charms' blight ;
We deem not lovely things can die,
    They look so heavenly and so bright.

The breath that bids its pulses sleep,
    Pales the sweet lip, and sinks the eye ;
But while we gaze, and gaze and weep,
    We dare not think it e'er can die.

Like love's young dream we see it fade,
    But 'tis so charming as it flies,
We follow still the lovely shade,
    And hope may droop, but never dies.

Too quickly fade our loveliest things,
  And stars will set and moons will wane,
But is't in the heart's imaginings
  That they will never shine again?

———

TIME HAS PASSED O'ER HIM.

(AN IMITATION.)

TIME has passed o'er him like a breeze
  Which steals sweet odours from the flowers,
As floating o'er the blossomed trees,
It but exhales their essences
  To give them to the perfumed hours.

Time has passed o'er him like a ray
  Which travels from the central sun,
Making, to all around it, day,
Brightening and warming in its way
  All that it rests or shines upon.

Time has passed o'er him like a mist,
  Which for awhile obscured the sky;
But, rising from the earth it kissed,
Found the bright light which here it missed,
  And shines a sun-lit cloud on high.

SONGS.

NELLY BROWN.

SWEET Nelly Brown, of Tawstock town,
   Was but a cotter's daughter,
But dukes might praise her pretty ways,
   And princes might have sought her.
Her honeyed lip a bee might sip,
   A sylph might praise her form,
Her eye was bright as sunshine light,
   Her cheek as sunshine warm.
O love, love, love, if any one you know,
   Who refuses your sceptre to own ;
You might rule him with a straw, if only once he saw
   The face of my sweet Nelly Brown.

By Taw's green side, 'twas there I spied
   This pride of Tawstock village ;
To Barum town was mother gone,
   And father to his tillage.
One rapturous look I scarcely took,
   My heart to hers had flown ;

I sighed " relent "—she sighed " content,"
  And mine was Nelly Brown.
O love, love, love, if any one you know,
  Who refuses your sceptre to own ;
You might rule him with a straw, if only once he saw
  The face of my sweet Nelly Brown.

THE COTTAGE OF THE YEO.

I KNOW the greenest, loveliest spot
  Of all this green and lovely isle,
And there I know a lowly cot
  Which would from palaces beguile :
'Tis fragrant with the spicy sighs
  Which, nestling, lurk among the flowers,
Till, fanned by bees' wings, they arise,
  And for the cottage leave the bowers.

And by the cottage flows a stream,
  Which dimples into smiles each hour ;
Uncertain which to woo, the beam
  Of sun above, or neighbouring flower :
And, as it passes the dear spot,
  It seems awhile to linger by ;
Ah, happy stream to watch that cot,
  " No meddling world inquiring why."

Oh ! could you see at twilight's hour,
    When eve its first soft dimness throws
The halo round the rich sunflower,
    The softened tints of the red rose ;
You then would sigh, as I have sighed,
    In these secluded walks to go ;
To leave the city's foolish pride
    For the sweet cottage of the Yeo.

Why does the flaunting city fling
    A glittering chain around my heart,
When I would be a lowly thing,
    And but sustain the humblest part ?
Honours and wealth, I seek ye not ;
    With you I joy should never know ;
This is my one dear, chosen spot,
    The lowly cottage on the Yeo.

THE YOUNG KNIGHT.

THE bugle is heard from the castle wall,
    And banners are seen by the castle gates ;
" Rouse, young knight, rouse at thy honour's call ;
    Thy helmet is brought, and thy palfrey waits."
Thus sang the minstrel through the hall,
And the young knight roused at the minstrel's call.

The knight was checked by a snow-white hand,
　And a voice like music breathed out, "Stay,
Oh, stay to protect thy native land !
　Not honour nor duty now calls thee away."
But the voice of the minstrel was heard in the hall,
And the young knight roused at the minstrel's call.

The young knight left his weeping bride,
　And a happy home and a honest name,
And poured out his proud heart's crimson tide,
　In the fatal search for a warrior's fame.
The voice of the minstrel was heard in the hall,
But it was to mourn over the young knight's fall !

―――

OH, DRY THOSE TEARS.

OH, dry those tears, those pearly tears,
　Which now thine eyes are steeping ;
Oh, drive those weak, those woman's fears,
　Which set thine heart a-weeping :
I ne'er, dear girl, could prove untrue,
　Your charms would never let me ;
How could I love a maid but you,
　How could I e'er forget thee ?

No ! If a smile from Beauty's eye,
    With luring bait, address me,
Then I shall heave a heartfelt sigh,
    And think upon my Jessy.
And should I tread on danger's ground,
    And pleasure's lures beset me,
Oh, then to thee my thoughts will bound,
    I shall not then forget thee !

RESTING TIME.

See, see, dear, the red sun is setting,
    And darkness, love's day-time, descends with its
    blessings,
The cares of the sunlight the world is forgetting,
    And its toil is repaid by the evening's caressings.
        Cease, cease, busy head, now,
        Thy worktime is sped now ;
        Cease, cease, nimble finger,
        Nor wearily linger,
The daylight is dying, its work is nigh done ;
And evening, blest life-time of love, is begun.

Turn, turn, dear, thine eyes from day's duty,
    Leave their dull task-work, and turn them on me ;
Labour surrenders the world, love, to beauty,
    The bird seeks its nestlings, and so, dear, must we.

Hands miss their mark, love,
When plied in the dark, love;
The wearisome day-time
Now gives way to play-time;
For the evening proclaims that day's task-work is done,
And the heart and the lip say their life is begun.

SONG.

WHEN sparkles the first star of eve in the sky,
Give a moment, dear Jessy, to me,
And think while you gaze on the twinkler that I
    Am then gazing and thinking on thee.
In the day for an instant your image may leave
    The warm throne where it ever should reign ;
But, ah ! at the love-breathing zephyrs of eve
    I think on my Jessy again.

Oh ! eve is the time for all beauty and bliss,
    They seem to recede from the sun,
But at eve the bright god gives his Thetis a kiss,
    And the sweet reign of love is begun.
And though in the day e'en such bosoms as ours
    Must from fondness or feeling refrain,
Yet evening, dear Jessy, has left us its hours
    To think on each other again.

LUCY GRAY.

BEWITCHING Lucy Gray,
  See youthful lovers two,
Enchained by you to-day,
  For your decision sue;
A willing prisoner
  For life is either beau;
Decide which you prefer,
  And let the other go.

One offers golden store,
  And houses, gems, and land;
The other is but poor,
  But comes with heart and hand:
Your choice, then, don't defer,
  Pronounce a yes or no;
Decide which you prefer,
  Or else *they both will go.*

SONG.

YOUNG Love on the breast
  Of a fair lily lighted,
Its snowy charms pressed,
  And sang there, delighted;

But the young flower, frighted,
From his bright gaze withdrew,
And the gay boy, slighted,
To another blossom flew.

Round a rose-tree near
A jasmine was clinging,
And profusely there
Was its fragrance flinging;
And young Love, springing,
Reached the jasmine flower,
And still kept singing,
As pleased as before !

———

SONG.

Young Love, when he flies,
In tears dips his wings,
And his heart's first sighs
Around him he flings.
The sad tear may dry,
Forgotten be the sigh,
For if once Love fly,
He his farewell sings.

Farewell !

A beautiful breast
  Love seeks in the spring,
And builds there his nest,
  Like a foolish thing :
He may cling there and sigh
Till his young hopes die ;
But if once Love fly,
  Then his farewell sing.

> Farewell !

———

SONG.

WE saw each other but an hour,
  But what has time with love to do?
An instant wakes the passion's power,
  And following years but prove it true :
Let duller souls than ours proclaim
  That time must fan Love's spark divine ;
A moment lights the brightest flame
  That ever glowed on any shrine.

We saw each other but an hour
  Beneath the soft, the moonlit sky;
Could years of truth exceed the power,
  Sweet Jessy, of your maiden sigh ?

10 *

The thrilling touch, the heaving breast,
  The sinking sigh, when sighs are true,
The birth of love, when love is blest,
  Oh ! what have these with time to do ?

———

LILLA'S LEGACY.

My pretty little Lilla's dead—
  At least is dead to me—
But ere her gentle spirit fled,
  She left a legacy ;
She left me—days of countless sighs
  And years of sweet regrets,
A love, alas ! which never dies,
  A heart which ne'er forgets.

I, kneeling, asked a single word
  In token of her love ;
Alas ! my prayer was never heard,
  Her cold lips did not move.
" Leave me but hope, alas !" I cried,
  " If more you cannot leave :"
She trembled, pressed my hand, and sighed,
  Say, should I smile or grieve ?

RIDDLE-ME-REE.

RIDDLE-ME-REE, Riddle-me-ree,
I love one and one loves me ;
'Tisn't for beauty, 'tisn't for pelf,
But each loves each for its own dear self ;
'Tisn't for this, 'tisn't for that,
And neither can say or think for what.
Riddle-me-ree, Riddle-me-ree,
What do I love, and what loves me ?

Riddle-me-ree, where should lips meet ?
Riddle-me-ree, where should hearts beat ?
Lips meet of course where others are meeting,
Hearts beat of course where others are beating ;
What do I wish for, what do I sigh for ?
What do I live for, what would I die for ?
Riddle-me-ree, Riddle-me-ree,
What do I love, and what loves me ?

———

SONG.

THE Torridge flows gently among its green valleys,
    And sings to the woods as it ripples along ;
The wood-dove coos over its musical waters,
    Where twitters the skylark its gladdening song.

But how can I list to the music around me,
  Or gaze on the charms it invites me to view?
Dejected, I dare not reflect on such beauties,
  Alas! I must bid them a joyless adieu.

No more must I sing on the bank of the Torridge,
  Waiting Echo's reply from the opposite shore;
Ah! no; I must leave the sweet stream in its windings,
  And list to the dreams of my fancy no more.
No more view the sun to The Wooder declining,
  And tinging the wave with its mellowing hue;
No more hear the low bells of Bideford chiming,
  Alas! I must bid them a joyless adieu.

Bear gently, sweet Torridge, these tears to my fair one,
  But, ah! that such weakness is mine never tell,
Breathe softly, young breeze, this adieu to my charmer,
  But say not who whispers so sad a farewell.
Farewell, ye loved hills, and farewell, ye loved valleys,
  Already ye seem to recede from my view;
Dejected, I dare not reflect on your beauties,
  Alas! I now bid them a joyless adieu.

LOVE IN EXCELSIS.

Oh, how I love !   Oh, how I love !
    Fondly as ever loved a swain ;
And she I love, and she I love,
    As fondly does she love again !
Then all who love rejoice with me ;
Love should not unrequited be,
But lips should meet in kisses sweet,
And hearts with hearts responsive beat.

Unblest by love—unblest by love,
    I passed unmoved the chilly hours ;
I heard no music from the grove,
    I saw no beauty in the flowers :
Life was a long dull wintry night,
    I neither pleasure felt nor pain ;
But life is now one quick delight,
    I love ! and I am loved again.

———

WRITTEN TO OLD MUSIC.

A gentle star once went astray,
    For why there is no telling,
And shed its mild and pleasant ray
    Upon my humble dwelling ;

It was a star that lit my path
    When it was dark and dreary ;
It was a solace to my heart
    When it was sad and weary.

The star resumed its native sphere,
    Which brightened at its shining ;
And soon my troubled sky was clear,
    My cloud had silver lining :
I thank the star which lit my path
    When it was sad and dreary ;
And bless the sweet but transient smile
    Which cheer'd my heart when weary.

THE STORM.

WE sat upon the pebble ridge,
    Close by the bounding sea,
And oft I gazed upon my love,
    And oft she gazed on me ;
And never smiled the leaping main
    So sweetly at the storm,
And never shall I love again
    So wildly or so warm.

We sat upon the pebble ridge,
  And there declared our love,
And all was passionate below
  And beautiful above :
How the delicious moments flew,
  We knew but love's sweet power,
We took the moments pleasure threw,
  Nor looked beyond the hour.

We sat upon the pebble ridge,
  And heard the breakers roar,
And oft my charmer told her love,
  And oft of truth I swore.
The wild winds sang around our head,
  The waves rolled at our feet,
Romantic love ne'er formed a bed
  More wild, more purely sweet.

We sat upon the pebble ridge,
  The time flew swiftly on,
And oft we wondered why so soon
  That eve of bliss was gone.
But suns, alas ! have slowly set,
  Since last I saw her form,
And never can my heart forget
  Our farewell in the storm.

HARVEST SONG.

THANK God for the harvest, the earth, as of yore,
Has yielded a rich, an all-bountiful store ;
Man ploughed, and man scattered the seed in the sod,
And in confidence left the sure increase to God ;
And God sent the frost to distend the rich soil,
To spare the stout ploughman full half of his toil;
And God sent the dews down, and God sent the rain,
And God sent the sunshine to ripen the grain.

> CHORUS.—Thank God for the harvest !

We have sown, we have reaped, we have garnered the yield,
Be it blest in the barn as 'twas blest in the field ;
The part that is owed, may the owner possess it ;
The part that is ours, to our use may God bless it !
And let us remember that part of the store
Belongs to the aged, the sick, and the poor :
To their use be the part that belongs to them blest,
And we pray that God's blessing will fall on the rest.

> CHORUS.—Thank God for the harvest !

THE ROSEBUD.

ENCUMBERED oft with pressing dews,
  The rosebud droops in seeming sorrow,
Yet soon resumes its former hues,
  Nay, blooms more beauteous on the morrow.
So love, though oft depressed by fears,
  And doomed awhile to sigh and languish,
Will yet shake off its dewy tears,
  And bloom the sweeter for its anguish.

SONG.

HAVE I found it ? Yes, yes, 'tis a heart,
            A young warm heart !
With the jewel I never can part,
            No, never can part !
There may be doubtless many who prize
The laughing light of beautiful eyes,
And some who say ruby, pouting lips,
All other beauties and charms eclipse :
        Eyes may bless,
        Lips may press,
But they're nothing without the heart.

Oh ! when you find a heart,

      A warm true heart,

With the treasure never part,

      Never, never part !

Eyes may grow dim as they grow old,

And even ruby lips become cold,

But hearts once touched with the holy flame

Of love are ever and ever the same ;

      And eyes will bless,

      And lips will press,

When they're bid to do so by the heart.

THE PROPHETIC BOAT.

> " Those only can tell
> Who have loved as young hearts can love so well,
> How the pulses will beat, and the cheek will be dyed
> When they have some LOVE AUGURY tried."
>
> L. E. L.

I'LL form a little boat

    And give it to the gale,

A cork shall be its float,

    An ivy-leaf its sail.

      Sing heigh-ho willow,

      My boat is on the billow.

Steadily, sweet boat, glide,
    And prithee, backward turn,
Borne homeward by the tide,
    Foretell my love's return.
          Sing heigh-ho willow,
          My boat is on the billow.

Bright did the moonbeams play,
    My hopes as brightly shone,
But ah ! that last sad ray
    Showed bark and hopes are gone.
          Sing heigh-ho willow,
          The grave shall be my pillow.

LIBERTY.

1830.

SHALL the bird fly from tree to tree ?
    Shall the beast roam from wood to wood ?
Shall finny wanderers cleave the sea,
    And revel in the briny flood ?
Shall these—shall nature all be free,
And only man want liberty ?

Man has the eagle's daring soul,
    The lion's great and generous heart ;
Search land and sea from pole to pole,
    Man is great Nature's noblest part.

Nature was made for man, but he,
Alone of all, wants liberty !

Alas, all nature lives on prey,
    Each hunts a weaker creature down ;
Brute feeds on brute, except that they
    Seek other kinds and spare their own.
Man follows man !   The weakest flee,
And yield their life, their liberty.

Curse on the cravens !   Whither fly?
    The flying wretch must be a slave ;
Thou or thy tyrant, man, should die,
    Thy footprint, see ! marks out his grave.
Strike now the blow !   Who dies? 'tis he !
Take thy reward—'tis Liberty.

TO THE TRICOLOUR.

1830.

Up with the flag of Liberty,
    Up with the white, the blue, the red,
Pay honour to the sacred three
    For which our fallen friends have bled.

We offer Freedom's foes the white,
    We seek not war, but *must* be free ;
Refused, we to the blue unite,
    And steep our hands, deep-red, in thee.
        Up with the three
        Bright tints of liberty,
The white, the red, and the true blue—
'Tis Freedom's flag !   Let all be true.

Wave till the foes of Freedom fall,
    Till comforts reach the poor man's cot,
Wave o'er the proud's devoted hall,
    And traceless leave the hated spot ;
Come, plant it here, no fitter place
    Than where the poor have been oppressed ;
Each flag waves o'er a ruin-trace,
    A traitor's home, a tyrant's nest.
        Up with the three
        Bright tints of liberty,
The white, the red, and the true blue :
'Tis Freedom's flag !   Let all be true.

TWO THOUSAND YEARS AGO.

TOWARDS the great, the wise, and good,
  We sometimes deem the progress slow ;
But let us think how the world stood
  About two thousand years ago.
Though we, a poor short-sighted race,
  Deem a long term two thousand years,
How insignificant the space
  In the wide range of Time appears !

Two thousand years ago !   Just when
  " Great Julius " heard that o'er the waves
There was an isle where savage men
  Ate acorns, and who dwelt in caves.
On Colne's and a few sedgy banks,
  Were some poor towns which scarce had names,
And a few huts, in feeble ranks,
  Fringed the wide marshes of the Thames.

Then Cromlechs and gaunt Druid rings
  From Kent to Sarum held their fires,
And men, at once their priests and kings,
  Harshly controlled our savage sires.

An unknown God demanded then
    Man's blood in bloody rites to flow ;
No GOD OF LOVE was known to men
    A short two thousand years ago.

Just then " the mighty Julius fell,"
    And while "Augustus taxed the world"
To us a Child was born, and hell
    Was countless fathoms deeper hurled.
And at the very instant rose
    London ! the central dwelling-place
Of men born to subdue God's foes,
    And publish to the world His grace.

The wondrous city was at first
    But a misshapen mass of wall,
Yet in the uncouth heap was nursed
    The spirit that must rule us all.
To London came the blest decree
    Which swelled the sun-lit arc above,
The Christian Land of Liberty
    Shall preach the Christian mission—" LOVE."

Heaven moves not as we creatures move,
    By impulses now good, now ill ;
God's ways are always ways of love,
    But His own times His plans fulfil.

Two thousand years ago high Heaven
    Proclaimed redemption's world-wide plan ;
Two thousand more perhaps are given
    To the wide-wandering tribes of man.

Evil and good in mighty war
    With us as with the world have fought,
Ill sometimes has eclipsed our star,
    The bright, the morning star of thought.
But clouds and darkness, and their powers,
    Though sometimes striving for the sway,
Will soon recede.   It must be ours
    To be dispensers of the day !

O England !   "To thyself be true,"
    Each idol in thy camp throw down ;
One Book, one Priest, one God in view,
    Take up at once thy cross and crown.
Error may strive, but strives in vain,
    Thou sword and crozier may'st defy ;
O'er thee the King of kings shall reign
    In never-failing dynasty.

THE GRAVE OF MY HOUSEHOLD.

PARTING.

I TREAD the beaten path again
  Which leads to where my household lie :
  The oldest of the hearts which sigh,
Again I head the sable train.

The young, the middle-aged, the old,
  Already sleep in this, their bed :
  I soon must bow my silvered head,
This is in each fresh sculpture told.

The anguish of my fevered brow,
  The breast which heaves, the eyes which weep,
  Seek solace in that solemn sleep ;
I almost pray, " Let it be now."

With weakened will, with bending form,
  Each day some little duties drop ;
  And soon the frail machine will stop,
And give its fibres to the worm.

Thus the slight flower and statelier tree
  Fall to the earth from which they sprung ;
  So nobler lips than mine have sung :
" As it hath been, so it must be."

11 *

THE FINAL HOME.

MEETING.

WITH decent rites, while grief o'erflows,
    We treasure up our brother's dust,
    And with the blessed and the just
It rests, like them, in calm repose.

The well-known thrice-repeated sound,*
    And creaking of the lowering rope
    We scarcely heard, for words of hope
Seemed then to fall from heaven around.

We looked down with a long, long glance,
    But scarcely saw terrestrial things,
    For Faith soared on exultant wings,
And all seemed to us as a trance.

We checked our sighs and dried each tear,
    For, gazing on the coffin lid,
    An angel said, as one once did,
" You must not seek your brother here.

" Lo ! he is risen and gone before."
    Give decent sorrow its full scope,
    But sorrow not as without hope :
You soon will meet to part no more.

* " Earth to earth, ashes to ashes, dust to dust."

A BURIAL IN THE SAND.

(A RECOLLECTION.)

STROLLING on Scarbro' sands one day,
I watched some little groups at play;
And one, whose sizes rose by grades,
Had all their tiny sea-side spades.

Two charming girls and three sweet boys,
Made the air ring with their shrill noise,
As in strange shapes uprose the sand
At these young engineers' command.

A castle, with wide moat around;
A spire, full three feet from the ground;
A breakwater to stem the tide;
All these, and many more were tried.

Till, tired with work, the elder-grown
At full length on the beach lay down,
And bade the young ones, for a whim,
Heap up the ground to cover him.

The youthful sextons' busy hands
Soon buried feet and arms in sand;
And the well-patted bank arose
And covered all but eyes and nose.

As thus he lay beneath the cliff,
With rigid limbs and body stiff,
It really might appear to all
Some shipwrecked sailor's funeral.

So like a grave the form they kept,
I could almost have o'er it wept:
So silent round it was their tread,
One might suppose their brother dead.

This lasted but a little while,
For soon up-springing with a smile,
The grave-sand which he shook away
Flew round his form like shining spray.

A joyous family again :
And, passed their mimic show of pain,
It makes me think, as here I stand,
What *is* a burial in the sand !

THE SUMMERS OF LONG AGO.

(WRITTEN BY COMMAND.)

" THE summers of long ago,"
   Why boast of them as bright?
The present summer, we know,
   Is quite as warm and bright.

The air is just as soft, ?
  The blossoms are as gay ;
The lark sang then aloft,
  He sings aloft to-day.

In summers of long ago
  You were a lovely child ;
In summers of later glow,
  You were a romper wild ;
Summers have since, we know,
  Ripened each early charm ;
And many must come and go,
  Ere time will their power disarm.

With never-ceasing flow
  The glittering sand-streams pass,
And brighten with their glow
  Time's double-apexed glass.
Glide on, dear shining stream,
  Flow on, bright moments, flow ;
Ye form as pleasant a dream
  As the summers of long ago.

PAPER DOLLS.

My sister Susan, long ago,
Indeed a score of years or so,
Among her nick-nacks and her " follies "
Possessed two charming paper dollies.
Prized far beyond all other toys,
They were her pets, companions, joys :
They were her world !   The world to her
Showed nothing then she would prefer.
I know not why : among the "may-be's,"
Perhaps she thought them really babies !
But years passed on, and my sweet Sue
From child and girl to woman grew ;
And toys and dolls were laid aside
For woman's cares and woman's pride.

I have not named that, years long back,
Susan grew up with Cousin Jack ;
John was but just a little older,
In fact, dear Susan reached his shoulder
They had the same pursuits and follies,
And both together nursed these dollies ;
But I've already said that Sue
Grew up to know a thing or two ;

Became in course of time a wife,
And passed a very pleasant life,
In washing limbs and brushing curls
Of three real boys and two fine girls.

Ah ! would that Jack, when he left Sue,
Had left off nursing dollies, too ;
Had left all paper trivialities,
And lived, like Susan, on realities !
But no !   Throughout long years of trade
He countless paper " dollies " made ;
Dolls of all sorts and forms and sizes,
And in all possible disguises.
He scarcely had a friend to call on,
But he would fix a paper doll on ;
Until at last his frightened neighbours
Returned upon him his life's labours ;
The long, the short, the large, the small,
Crowded upon him, one and all;
They came from all parts of the town,
And weighed poor bankrupt Johnny down :
Broke with their heavy weight his back,
And made an end of Cousin Jack.

WASHING DOLLY.

" Hoov dot a bit ov dirt on oos nose ;
    I mus' waas oos ittle face, I s'pose,
    Oo naughty dal !   Oov don an' dot
    Up on oos nose a dait back spot."
(So Minnie talked to her doll, who was drest,
As dollies always are, in their best.)

    " I 'clare I mus' det de sponge an' tub,
        An' div' oos dirty ittle face a rub ;
        Don't ty !   Oo sal be my keen ittle daughter
        When I've was't oos face in de nice soap and
            water."
(I could not help smiling at Minnie's folly,
When thus she determined to wash her dolly.)

    " Was'-a-face, was'-a-face, make a face keen,
        Dolly s'all have a face fit to be seen,
        Stub-off and dub-off a dirt from oos stin,
        Dolly's face s'al be as keen as a pin."
(I began to feel sorry a washing so brief,
And for such a small spot, should bring dolly to grief.)

    " Oh, dolly, dear dolly !   Oh, where are oos lips?
        An' oos 'ed cherry cheeks an' oos nose's 'ed
            tips ?

Oh, where, dolly dear, is each pitty boo eye?
Oh, I've dubbed them all off! I must sit down
    and ky!"
(I'm afraid if each washed off his dear pet's sweet follies,
We should lose half the charms of our "grown-up"
    dollies.)

TO THE LADY MAY.

(———— VALE, BLACKHEATH.)

SWEETEST, dearest, happiest maiden,
Still with simplest virtue laden,
Pure as when thy first spring blossom
Hid blest fruitage in its bosom :
Thou pleasant, bright, sunshiny thing,
Early summer joining spring,
Like the fragrant orange-shoot,
Rich at once with bloom and fruit ;
Winsome, blithesome, joyous creature,
With content in every feature,
Save when hopes, supremely pleasant
Wrestle with the happy present ;
When a father's love and mother's—
Half-forgotten for another's—
Mingle, in delicious strife,
With rich hopes of future life,

As contends all earthly love,
With our promised bliss above.

    Maiden, while thy cheek still flushes
At each tender thought to blushes,
Checking purest hopes of blisses,
Even when lips melt to kisses;
While thy tears still know no sadness
But the precious dew of gladness,
Or the happy mixture starting
At each meeting and departing;
While thy friendships still preserving
With a fondness never swerving;
Lady, while blest wishes hover
O'er thee, of each friend and lover;
Though thy sire, in world-known verses,
All thy " baby charms" rehearses;
Yield to me the pleasant duty,
Thus to hint at ripened beauty :
Kindly read the verse I lay,
Low at thy feet, dear Lady May!

MY DAFFODILS.

Dear friend, I pray you, drop your quills,
And come to see my daffodils.
Leave books and bookshelves, desks and tills,
They're trash compared with daffodils.
Before the swallows show their bills
March winds have blown on daffodils,
The banks of streams, the sides of rills,
Have yielded up their daffodils.
What golden beauty flames and fills
My garden with gay daffodils!
Here all the fragrance which distils
A young Narcisse to daffodils;
And poetry for two idylls
You'll gather from my daffodils;
For dreadful Pluto, King of ills,
Snatched Proserpine from daffodils,
As " Dis's waggon " clomb the hills
And, " frightened, let fall " daffodils.

The thrush, while morning song he trills,
Sings but to praise my daffodils;
The nightingale its soft note stills,
Contemplating these daffodils;

The blackbird through my coppice shrills
Its clarion, shouting " daffodils ; "
The lark with keener transport thrills,
Enraptured by my daffodils.
The lambs which gambol on the hills
Might frisk through beds of daffodils,
Not grown in formal rows and drills,
But nature-planted daffodils !

You cannot hope on window sills
Of city homes such daffodils.
Misers may, sighing, tear their wills,
With all their many codicils,
To purchase half my daffodils.
Doctors should throw away their squills,
Juleps, confections, draughts, and pills,
Prescribing walks mid daffodils.
Drapers should leave lutestrings and twills,
And nothing sell but daffodils.
The chops, which one short minute chills,
And soups, and stews, and roasts, and grills,
A cook might leave for daffodils ;
And fishmongers their skates and brills
Might sell, uncleaned, both scales and gills,
And holiday with daffodils.
Painters should exercise their skills
In pictures of my daffodils.

Each "dimn'd old horse" in " dimn'd old mills"
Might change its track for daffodils,
And gladly leap between the thills
Of a cart filled with daffodils.
And topers, leaving sips and swills,
Taste purer joys with daffodils.
'Twould change the nature of gorils
To stay awhile with daffodils.
Oh, what are Gladstones and D'Isrils
To eloquence of daffodils ?
Without objections or cavils
All would prefer my daffodils.
Fairies might make stomacher frills
From my indented daffodils,
And pixies dance their light quadrilles
In the parterres of daffodils.

O flowers of March !   O gay Lent lils !
(But better known as daffodils)
O sweet narcissi ! sweet jonquils !
(Sweeter than all as daffodils !)
From bulb to stamen and pistils,
No flower can rival daffodils.
The rose, one morning frost which kills,
Compares not with March daffodils.
In vain will showery wet Aprils
Promise compeers with daffodils.

More fragrant than the best pastilles,
Or beds of aromatic dills,
Is essence of my daffodils.
How gracefully, when calm instils
The sleeping air, hang daffodils !
And when the breeze its charge fulfils,
How proudly wave my daffodils ! ˙
The " cup of joy," though brimming, spills
No atom, filled with daffodils.
A perfect cure for blue devils
Laughs out from beds of daffodils.
Why, twenty Mary Somervilles
Might science leave for daffodils ;
And honey-seeking, gay trochils
Might make their nests in daffodils.

So come at once !   No " wait untils."
All things besides are utter " *Nils*,"
Compared with priceless daffodils.
A week's delay quite imperils
The sight of sights, my daffodils !

P.S. Expect no fare but plain lentils,
And "*Rus in Urbe*" daffodils.

LOVE'S CALENDAR.

JANUARY.

Mid frost and snow first breathed the new-born year,
  And smiled, though with a shade of melancholy;
But when I saw the Crocuses appear,
I gave them welcome with a loving cheer:
              Perhaps 'twas folly.

FEBRUARY.

A month soon passed, and lo! a Virgin white
  Rose from the snow with the cold grace of meekness;
Joy fluttered through my heart at the first sight;
'Twas love, I think, but am not certain quite:
              Perhaps 'twas weakness.

MARCH.

With the pale crescent of another moon
  Desire's own flower, the languid Daffodilly,
Waved in the meadows, March's golden boon:
I was a captive to its beauty soon:
              Perhaps 'twas silly.

APRIL.

Then the moist month of the sad Violet
   Showed the pale Primrose in faint fragrance dying;
And soon my sympathising eyes were wet—
Wet with love's precious tears, I thought ! 'Twas yet,
               Perhaps, vain sighing.

MAY.

Soon sunny May glistened with radiant morns,
   And bright Anemonés, in silver patches,
Peeped through the grass tufts. Plucking May's
   " new-borns,"
I soon got wounded with the haw's sharp thorns;
               Perhaps mere scratches.

JUNE.

June brought the Rose, the ever-wondrous Rose ;
   I felt it was the very flower I wanted :
In vain around me varied beauty blows,
O'ercome by one supremely, I suppose,
               Perhaps enchanted.

JULY.

Then bloomed the honey-bearer of July,
   Weighed down with fulness of its own rich sweetness.
I quite enjoyed the luscious luxury,
But touched the border of satiety,
               Perhaps repleteness.

AUGUST.

Dazed by the brilliance of the " Floral Sun,"
   I bowed before that mass of yellow burning;
Fixing my gaze from morn till day was done,
Turning and turning, as its wheel went on,
                            Perhaps o'erturning.

SEPTEMBER.

Then weedling Poppies shimmered through the wheat,
   Like rubies through a mesh of golden netting :
I soon admired the beautiful deceit,
My former loves, no longer at their feet,
                            Perhaps forgetting.

OCTOBER.

Anon, the wild's own flower, the purple Heath,
   O'er the wide moor to winter's music dances ;
So freely ring its wind-swung bells beneath
The scattered furze, the joy intense I breathe
                            Perhaps entrances.

NOVEMBER.

The golden Gorse-bloom then its perfume pours,
   Proclaiming lover's bliss not out of fashion.
Oh ! what a tale for the cold wintry hours !
I loved it ! 'Tis my pet of all the flowers,
                            Perhaps my passion.

DECEMBER.

December last.   His dear old white head crowned
  With fadeless wreath of scarlet-berried Holly :
I loved that, too ! and on reflecting, found
I had been loving all the full year round !
                              This can't be folly.

THE MUSIC OF THE YEAR.

PROEM.

A HYMN, thrice blessëd, hailed December's close,
"Glory to God, and earth's long-hoped repose."
After that angel-song of promised peace,
Music, perfected, seems awhile to cease ;
And now a solemn stillness reigns above,
Crowning accomplished harmony and love.

JANUARY.

The placid sky is silent.   But, yet, hark !
Methinks I hear, in tremulous notes, the Lark
Attempting music as he " upward springs
A little way," and in soft rapture sings.
Echo must sure the angel-hymn prolong,
His ti-ri-la is still of love the song.

FEBRUARY.

Midst sunshine glimpses in the length'ning days
Earth's small musicians tune their tender lays.
The Linnet and the Sparrow chirp to prove
Nothing so small to be denied its love.
Even the Titlark and the tiny Wren
Share in the universal joy of men.

MARCH.

With louder notes cheers the unwearied Thrush,
His mate close sitting in the hawthorn bush;
And the bright Goldfinch, clad in red and gold,
Leaves not its sweet melodious tale untold.
There's not a clump of budding underwood
But pours out music to some tiny brood.

APRIL.

From scorching climes, towards the tempering north
The early Swallows come, and twitter forth
The pleasant music of their sweet unrest,
Building beneath our gabled eaves their nest;
And the lush Blackbird, whistling loud and strong,
Proclaims his ardent rapture in his song.

MAY.

Now, midst the snowy blossoms of the May,
The wandering Cuckoo "sings both night and day,"

And through the woods the plaintive monotone
Calls the unmated not to live alone.
The tall bird-palaces of every grove
Hide new-built homes of sweet parental love.

JUNE.

In the warm, bright, and blissful month of June
The queen of warblers perfecteth her tune,
As through the love-fraught eve, and all night long,
The Bird of Night pours out her loving song;
And the soft notes tell such a moving tale,
That listening maids with tenderness grow pale

JULY.

Before the ending of the hot July,
Away the Swallow and the Cuckoo fly,
And to Italian and Egyptian groves
Carry the sweet remembrance of their loves;
And, haply, there throughout each sultry night,
To dusky beauty chaunt some new delight.

AUGUST.

As the stout reaper, with his swinging scythe,
Mows down the cereal stems, upright yet lithe,
He well can tell how the defended nest
Holds a protector of each unfledged breast;
And as the screeching mother mounts on high,
Her grand despairing love-notes fill the sky.

SEPTEMBER.

Not yet is music past ; the song of love
Is daily cooed by the domestic dove ;
Alike in nature's lichen-studded domes,
And the dull planking of provided homes,
From bush, from tree, it pours into the skies
Its love—'tis love with all its joys and sighs.

OCTOBER.

The stars, love's cressets, still as brightly burn,
But day and night's musicians, in their turn,
Each having taught some listening lover's ear
Their music-lesson of the circling year,
Leave the charmed hearer in a pensive mood,
To the all-conquering power of love subdued.

NOVEMBER.

Still, on the Robin's crimson-tinted breast
Is the ne'er-dying warmth of love exprest ;
And as in winter's coldest days some springs
Still warmly flow, so he in winter sings ;
And many a note, from rushy stream and mere,
Completes the loving music of the year.

DECEMBER.

Hark to the hymn by angels sung again !
Still love, a Father's love, is the refrain.

Join, man and beast, and all ye joyous birds
Supply fit music for the blessed words !
Let the loud chorus soar to bliss above—
To the Great Parent, to each creature LOVE !

THE WISHING-CAP.

IN a morning walk, by a lucky hap
I found Fortunatus's wishing-cap ;
And every one knows when he wears this hat
He has only to wish, and the thing comes pat ;
So I thought, as I put on this wonderful " tile,"
" O what shall I wish ?   I must think awhile."
Wealth ?   Well, I scarcely had uttered the word,
When it came in a bulk which was quite absurd :
There were heaps of silver and heaps of gold :
I don't know the sum, for it never was told.
But wealth only brought me food, clothes, and a hovel,
And these I could earn with a pick-axe and shovel ;
And finding it coupled with cares not a few,
I said, " Wealth, be off ! " and away it flew.
I reflected a bit, and had just whispered " Station ! "
When down dropped the crown of a new-made nation ;
It seemed exactly to fit my head,
But gold is heavier far than lead :
So I soon got rid of the crown with a fling,
And I pity the man who succeeds me as king !

Then I thought upon Fame; and her trumpet blowing
Just set for a moment my spirits a-glowing;
But neglecting my virtues they praised my vice,
And so I declined to buy Fame at its price;
And I thoroughly scorned the penny trumpet
Of the saucy, heartless, lying strumpet.
So I took off the hat, and began to ponder,
What is the real use of the night-cap yonder?
The good that is likely to come with a wish
Is no proper food for beast, bird, or fish;
I'd rather buy with a well-earned groat
A slice from a loaf or first inch of a coat—
I'd rather dig on from morning to night,
And eat my spare crust with a good appetite,
Than be stuffed with dainties, and clothed in flimsies,
And die of a lengthened attack of the whimsies.
I can wish—Now that horrible hat is gone,
I suppose I may safely and rightly wish on;
For every wish with its work I will tether,
And wishing and working shall both go together.
I wish, then, as much plain food as I earn;
Of knowledge as much as I strive to learn;
As much of all good as I fairly deserve,
When blest by the God whom I try to serve.
Be it little or much, I am sure it will prove
That I owe the chief part to His kindness and love!

A BEAUTIFUL HAND.

LORD CHARLES has a beautiful hand,
   And of gloves a most beautiful pair,
So small and so delicate, and
   So exact, they both fit to a hair.

It is not a labourer's hand,
   Lord Charles does not work for his living:
His fingers, bejewell'd and grand,
   Know more of accepting than giving.

For his hand neither makes things nor mends,
   Works neither with mattock nor pen :
It begs from his family friends,
   Or borrows from commoner men.

Well ! I know a hand like a fist !
   It is firm, it is strong, it is big ;
It is honest from fingers to wrist,
   It can plash, it can prune, it can dig :

It ploughs, and it sows, and it reaps,
   Not caring for sores nor for aches,
And it don't leave its gettings in heaps :
   Each friend of its earnings partakes.

It works for a wife, girl and boy;
   It rocks a young baby to sleep;
It hurrahs with true friends when they joy,
   It wipes off their tears when they weep.

It teaches the stupid and young;
   It helps the decrepit and poor;
It fights for the weak 'gainst the strong;
   And what would you have hands do more?

It spreads all around it delight;
   It brushes away all despair;
It does this from morning till night,
   And then it is lifted in prayer.

I call THIS a beautiful hand: .
   Who has such an one to extend,
Oh, thus let him honour me! And
   I'll grasp it as that of a friend.

DREAMS.

"Life is such stuff as dreams are made of."

A BABE lay in his mother's lap,
   And she sat doting on his smile,
Nor thought the rosy little chap
   Was dreaming baby dreams the while.

He dreamt of kisses warm and sweet,
    The round of childhood's every toy,
Then, trying his unpractised feet,
    He woke, and found himself a boy.

The boy then dreamed his boyish dreams
    Of long-spun essays, faction-fights,
Of honours gained by wondrous themes,
    Of half-imagined new delights.
The student-time so quickly flew,
    Scarce his curriculum began
Ere he was roused to duties new ;
    He woke and found himself a man.

Then manhood dreamt its dream of love,
    Of riches, station, pomp, and power ;
Each day for some new prize he strove,
    And in the striving fled the hour.
The daily dream was passing sweet,
    But soon awoke the ripened sage ;
The scenes had passed in changes fleet,
    Manhood had given place to age.

And age now dreams its blessëd dream
    Of warmer suns and brighter skies :
Sees an eternal glory beam
    On angels' lips, in angels' eyes;

Dreams of a Father's smiling face,
　　Heaven opening to the wondering view ;
We reach in dreams that glorious place :
　　When shall we wake and find it true ?

———

BIRTHDAY THOUGHTS.

BY A SEPTUAGENARIAN.

THE happy morn of childhood's spring
　　I passed 'midst wildling flowers,
And, like a lark upon the wing,
　　I carolled through the hours.
I well remember each sweet joy
　　Of that delightful season ;
I may have sighed while yet a boy,
　　But quite forget the reason.

A sunny sky blessed manhood's noon,
　　And I, delighted, prized it :
Mid-life, too, brought its pleasant June—
　　I'm sure I ne'er despised it.
There may have been a rainy day,
　　As passed the summer breeze on ;
If so, I wept my woes away,
　　And quite forget their reason.

And now I joy through winter's eve,
  Thankful for hours so pleasant ;
O'er no regretful past I grieve,
  Nor quarrel with the present.
Hope is the solace of my soul ;
  Distrust were surely treason ;
    I " Abba " cry, and on the whole,
  Think TRUSTING LOVE is reason.

W. F. R. *natus*, Jan. 29, 1802.

UNWIN BROTHERS, PRINTERS, CHILWORTH AND LONDON.

www.ingramcontent.com/pod-product-compliance
Lightning Source LLC
Chambersburg PA
CBHW031111020726
47495CB00007B/2152